The Gatekeeper's Daughter

Lucy Lamont

Published by Lucy Lamont, 2024.

This is a work of fiction. Similarities to real people, places, or events are entirely coincidental.

THE GATEKEEPER'S DAUGHTER

First edition. September 22, 2024.

Written by Lucy Lamont.

Chapter One

I grew up around antiquities, drawn to the ones in the glass cabinets that my mum would whisper used to belong to some long-lost dynasty or about the crest of an old mystical family. People had held those items and pressed their memories, wishes, or fears into them. What decisions had left their brass ornamentations and statuettes, or delicately created porcelain, abandoned in the hands of another?

It ached when these possessions didn't whisper their secrets back because my own were blurry. I was old enough to have a life of my own, but I had no passion of my own to share with mine. I was empty. When I was young, it was hard not to daydream about the details that Mum purposefully left out. I'd sit waiting at the built-in shelf at the back of the shop; Joanne had turned it into a small desk for me and my homework. Instead, whilst Mum catalogued or researched in between customers, I would wonder about the fabric of that hat or the missing clasp of that necklace, until she'd use tidbits of stories as carrots to make me finish my own work.

Joanne was like family by that point, she'd looked after me nearly as much as Mum herself since Dad wasn't in the picture. I remember it had still taken time, months, for me to be comfortable in her quaint antique shop. As far as they'd known, I hadn't remembered anything odd happening during my time there, but there were shadowed corners I still kept in my eye line. The shadows had noticed me in return one day, and I'd been too scared to turn my back on that corner again. I'd cried, but Mum and Joanne had assumed it was the recently acquired taxidermy.

At some point I was allowed to walk back from school alone, along our town's wide streets. Occasionally my friend Olivia would join me, and she chatted away the time, but I would still miss whispering with antique objects that passed through the shop.

I lived through school's daily drivel for the hours I got to explore and watch the world. I always said I was back home on time but as long as I was back before Mum, only Olivia was any the wiser. Our town was a hive; it was as if everyone I met there already knew what secrets they'd pass along to something sentimental, whilst I couldn't help but feel like the ghost those items left behind. The weight of the community spirit and local laughter felt heavy and exhausting, yet simultaneously helped me remember some of my own substance. There were a few long streets of eclectic shops that I enjoyed walking as I watched others browse before I headed back along the stony coast.

Mum had obviously picked this town on purpose, and whilst I couldn't imagine leaving, I longed to explore outside of what I already knew. Perhaps collecting different flavours would season me that little bit more. I knew she'd wanted me to feel content, at least satisfied, but those glimpsed shadows had left me with an imprint and all my days since seemed overcast. Along the way back home, I would pass the small office of the charity Mum had sought when she'd discovered my imprint. The purple door, tucked into the row of terrace houses, reminded me of my family's efforts to understand when, on occasion, I could see their fear of something lost reflected back at me. I regretted that it was all a pretence for me and, in avoidance of that agonising look of uncertainty, I held on to the questions about my father that I could have asked my mother.

When I finished school, Mum fell ill, and though our small-roomed house was our own curbside real estate, I couldn't afford to be philosophical about the contract that I traded my time with. I still miss Mum's stories.

Chapter

Two

I looked around the town where my search had left me. My van was still locked around me against the secrets outside. I had parked at a charming train station; the street went down towards some shops, and a slight slope revealed traditional residential roofs behind. There weren't many people around and everything looked familiar, though I couldn't recall being here before. I couldn't look at the white wooden lattice and medium-sized statue outside the station without seeing it again, faded in my memory. Taking my phone from its holder, I briefly looked at the rest of the directions before messaging Olivia.

I've arrived safe, I tapped, *but feeling déjà vu. Find me if you never hear from me again.*

I rummaged in the passenger footwell for my jacket and locked Rosie, my van, with a heavy clunk. My phone buzzed with Olivia's response.

Don't do anything I wouldn't do. I'm only at the end of the line! x

One of the more crushing burdens recently had been clearing through Mum's possessions. I couldn't bear the thought that someone else might whisper to these objects. It didn't take long for Olivia to connect my delaying tactics with my mother's affinity for memories, and so with my permission, she firmly set a date and helped me through it. Each box we sorted brought sorrow in its own way, as I couldn't bear to see those memories split up and lost. Among photo albums and bank statements, we found paperwork pertaining to things my mother had never spoken about and questions I had never asked. Money was tight when I was growing up, and yet, she'd secretly owned a house in this historic little town. It was the first time I realised I didn't know her as well as I'd thought, and I had to see it for myself.

I passed the row of shops where those people I'd seen minutes before were saying goodbye. Couples and the leisurely enjoyed their first brews or passing-the-time seconds whilst children were away at school. Shops, more independent than franchised, were open for the retired and the tourists. Though it was cloudy, I had to adjust my phone's brightness for the right turn. The streets grew grassier as I walked.

It hadn't taken me long to get through Mum's documents and, whilst I'd been waiting for the probate to go through, I worked towards having the means to visit. Rosie was more homely to me than our empty-small-roomed house, with her layers of blue throws that hung about my bed-sofa-and-wardrobe. My corner boudoir overlooked a small kitchen and through the cabin window and windscreen that guided where I went.

This week it led to a pleasant looking street, the buildings detached with a luxurious amount of space around them. Modestly sized trees lined the pavement and punctuated the grass that was languid from winter. The only reason I didn't feel the need to tidy my hair, to mitigate any suspicion that I was scouting the area out, was the fact that most of the residences were just as untidy. Yet even as I crossed the road to the decreasing house numbers of iron and wood, I wondered whether I should've thought more about what I might find here. At one hundred and twenty, my eyes skipped ahead, knowing instantly which front hedge was supposedly mine. One hundred and eighteen. One hundred and sixteen. I didn't know how long the house had been empty, but the garden wasn't as bad as I'd feared, and the rest of it didn't stand out among the street.

Without coat pockets, I grappled with my shoulder bag and had to rest it on a lichen covered wall to search for the unfamiliar keys. Weeds reached from between the paved stones that led to the door, whilst layers of past and present foliage pressed into the path. Strangely, ivy and mildew hadn't yet touched the house itself. Following up a single step, I thought it would be sensible to use the iron knocker before using my key. I gave the house a moment or two, as if preparing it before breaking its quiet reverence, and unlocked the door.

A loud, deep rumbling gave me pause when I peered into a dust-hazed hallway. A slender white figure crouched at the kitchen entrance. Dread made me focus on its pink, pointed ears and nose. My heart skipped that second. Its milky-blue eyes had known exactly where I was before I'd opened the door as surely as that deep warning rumble echoed from beneath its sculpted chest. I couldn't take in anything else from the stairs to the other rooms around me. Its narrow jaw raised and I couldn't help but watch its soft flecked nose decide our next reactions. I was torn between backing out the way I'd come to call someone, and waiting to see if I was deemed enough of a friend, when the choice was made for me. Its powerful haunches rippled as it walked carefully, crouched and tense like the reaper itself about to strike.

I jolted, suddenly thinking the first option was more sensible, when, just as I was about to close the door, she barked. A controlled alert. Her cold, intelligent eyes watched my movement, and her nose twitched, sniffing the air around me. I got the impression that backing down would be the worst thing I could do. I gave her the respect that a majestic creature would expect and avoided staring at her directly, though I kept watch from my peripherals. As she registered what I was doing, she sat back, watching me stoically. She was calm, all signs of her previous aggression could almost have been part of a fairy tale.

"Hello," I scarcely got out.

She remained a polite distance from the door, only shuffling forward when I couldn't decide who should make the first contact. She gave a gentle whine and nudge of her soft muzzle. I slowly raised my hand, open-palmed and relaxed, though my heart was beating double-time to make up for the ones it had missed. I was able to give her ear a quick scratch and twisted her collar around to find the attached gold pendant. Muscle memory whipped my phone out and found my keypad to dial the number as I read it.

I angled my body to prevent her from bolting, whilst she leaned her ear into my open palm in demand. The phone rang to the point I nearly hung up.

"Hello?" A deep, crackled voice made its way out the speaker.

"Hello," I quickly cleared my throat, "I... I think I have your dog at my house. I'd offer to bring her back, and can if you think she'll be okay, but I'm new to the area and..."

There was a long pause as I waited for the relieved response that I'd expected.

"My d—" I heard the realisation break through mid-sentence and wondered if this forgetfulness was why the dog had wandered. "White?"

"Yes, would you mind telling me her name?" Would she respond to the name he gave me?

"Of course, her name's Oona. I hope she's behaving okay."

"So far." I mirrored her inclined head. "Just a moment."

I held the phone away and attempted her name in a clear, commanding tone. She shuffled again, obviously listening.

It turned out the gentleman, Eoghan, was further up the street. Oona hadn't explored too far. She plodded beside me contently when I called her to follow while I looked for another house. The further we walked, the more comfortable I was that she wasn't going to bolt. Oona barely even glanced at the odd passing car and gradually the street became more rural. Space between the houses grew larger until country lanes spiralled off into nearby fields and brush.

When we arrived, the foliage decorated this house like clothing. Oona led the way and sat primly by the front door waiting for me; she clearly knew where she was supposed to be. The door opened as I made my way through the garden. Oona gave a patient little whine as her paws only just left the doorstep in excitement. The gentleman gave her fuss as he leaned one hand on his silver-topped cane. His crooked back straightened, and he looked at me. His face was weathered. Deep lines marked his eyes as if he'd been awake for too long, and his grey hair was cropped but combed back, his short beard was neglected.

"She has a mind of her own." He chuckled as Oona let herself in. "Thank you, Ms...?"

"Woods... Morgan, really. Does she do this often then? Isn't it dangerous for her to be wandering around?"

He maintained such a casual composure about his missing dog, I had to remember there were roads and people who wouldn't be so forgiving.

"Woods? You must be Peredur's daughter then?" He studied me a fraction too long with eyes like the blue sky above and then smiled. "Oona doesn't go far. Are you staying long, Miss Woods? Have you seen much of the town yet?" He adjusted his grip on his cane and gave the street a quick glance. I followed his look but saw nothing out of the ordinary. A single neighbour working in their garden. A flock of black birds dancing around the road.

I took a steady breath, uncertain of how much I should say. My thoughts were already shifting like sand. "I'm not sure yet to be honest. I'm just visiting for the time being."

He nodded and hummed. "Hundred and sixteen down the way? Forgive me, I knew your father. I was very sorry to hear of his passing."

I nodded in response, not really knowing what I could say that summed up the history with my father adequately. "Me too," I said, only too aware that the opportunity to know him was long gone. "Were you friends?"

"Practically family." The pain in his face reflected my own, and I thought maybe my misgivings could be paused until I had something more solid about my father to hold on to. Perhaps it was something in my own expression that echoed Eoghan's sentiment and made him invite me in, but it could've just as easily been loneliness.

Even though I felt for my phone in my pocket before stepping inside, a sense of calm fell over me. I felt safe here.

"I was just preparing some tea if you'd like any? I only have what I've picked locally I'm afraid, there's nothing quite like picking your own." He hobbled in, guiding me through to a large open room.

"Oh, I'm okay, thanks, but don't let me stop you." I looked around as he bent over a small tray of different shaped spouts. Oona had settled against the raised tiling of the fireplace, her eyes half closed but her ears twitching at every little sound, alert.

The room held a broad collection of leather-bound books, brass devices that I couldn't name, and labelled jam jars of dried plants and what may have been withered animal parts. The part of me that missed the shop wanted to disturb them and find out about this man's life, rather than my father's. He was evidently a collector and some kind of academic. Locked glass cabinets further in revealed more rows of timeworn spines and fine golden line-work chartered star systems on the ceiling above, but it was the huge framed painting above the fireplace that caught me. It was a city, catching the moment before the sun had fully risen, light glinting from distant windows and spires. A single vast bridge led traders over the surrounding canal and into a vibrant marketplace where there was a dance troop, mid-act, performing at its centre.

A sudden tinkling from a silver spoon caught my breath and the smell of spruce tea reached me as Eoghan eased himself into the armchair opposite me.

"So... how long did you know my father? Did you meet when one of you moved here?"

He rumbled, clearing his throat, the lines between his eyes deepened as if stirring his memories. "I actually knew Peredur as a boy; he grew up in that house. I was friends with his father first— we worked with the same people, and he used to help me pass love notes to my dear wife," he said, chuckling.

There were no photos, I noticed. Did he not wish to remember them or was it just too painful?

"When we came back here after travelling, my daughter was in search of her own life, and Peredur was a similar age by that point. He helped us out every now and then until he took over your grandfather's work... Do excuse me if this seems rather personal, but I take it you don't know much about your mother's side either?"

I blinked, resetting my eyebrows, as if something about my posture had given away more than I'd thought. In that moment, I realised he must have briefly known my mother too. Fresh loss built up in my throat, and I tried to clear the intruding memories.

I swallowed. "A little. Her parents passed away before I knew them, and she doesn't have any brothers or sisters to help out, if that's what you mean."

"I see." He nodded deeply, taking a sip of tea. "Well, I'm not much use for heavy lifting anymore but we'll happily help where we can, won't we Oona?"

As if understanding what Eoghan had offered on her behalf, one of Oona's pointed ears flicked in response.

"As much as I enjoy her company, you'll want to know that her real home is your father's house. Oh, I've been making sure she's got a bowl of something and that she keeps out of trouble, but she has a close bond with your family and knows her place is over there really."

It all made a little more sense, why she had returned there, and I realised I had misjudged the situation that brought me here. My gaze shifted back to Oona's lithe white figure to find her clear eyes watching me.

"I don't think that should be a problem," I said, unsure if these discoveries were still what I wanted, "though truthfully, I don't know how much time I'll have for her..."

"She's quite independent really, and, if you need me to, I'm happy to continue looking after her. She'll soon understand." Eoghan finished his tea, finally resting the cup on a table beside him. There was so much about my father's life that he might know, but only one immediate question burned my tongue.

I took a deep breath. "I understand if this was something my father never spoke about, but would you happen to know why my mother left with me? She didn't really talk about this place, so I assume there was something."

Sympathy traced Eoghan's frown, and I got the impression he was deciding how much was appropriate for me to know. If not me, who else would he tell?

"I'd hate for this to sound terribly cliched, but your parents still loved each other dearly. I could see it when Peredur spoke of you both. You had just begun to walk properly on your own when they must have decided it was for the best. As far as I know, your father's work simply overtook his life..." It looked as if he might continue for a moment before his shoulders raised in a small shrug.

It seemed too modest an explanation for the alternative life it had given us. Wisps of Mum working late and echoes of her whispered discussions with Joanne danced intangibly around me. There was something more. Perhaps it would've been too good to be true to know my father in one afternoon, and perhaps the house would know more.

"I understand." I nodded and paused for a moment. "What did he do? You said it was my grandfather's work?"

He cleared his throat again before making some uncertain murmurs. "He worked in travel, I believe. I can't say that either of them spoke to me much about it. It took up their time though, that's for sure, sometimes it was weeks between seeing them."

By the time I made my way back through the garden, I didn't know how much of the house I could confront. The clouds were illuminated, and the sky wore them like a cloak. A winter chill accompanied the wind. I couldn't wait any longer. I would shop for a few small items of food and move Rosie, but I had to at least look around the house. I walked through the weeds that reached from the paved stones, as my stomach reached up my throat. I pressed past the layers of foliage, as my heart pressed against my chest. I didn't knock this time; it had kept its secrets long enough.

Chapter
Three

The door opened easily, casting light between the pair of windows behind me and into the hallway. There was no guarding presence this time, Oona had followed me at a distance before she disappeared into another garden. I was greeted by a burgundy tiled floor that stretched past two closed rooms and some stairs. I closed the front door behind me and tried the immediate light switch. Light filtered into the rest of the hallway and I opened the first door on my right. The fading sun danced through the bushes outside and onto the sheets that covered its furniture... my furniture. It wasn't a small room, but it didn't span the width of the house like the kitchen. Gripping the edge of the sheet in front of the window, I pulled slowly to reveal the worn angles of a desk, its leather writing pad faded and its little drawers resistant from waiting. The other sheet figures in this room were taller, and I could imagine the pages they held even before I peeked. These weren't my things yet. Their familiarity belonged to someone long gone and every disturbance made me want to apologise for startling their peace, but also like I knew that someone a little more at the same time.

I passed the door that likely opened into the garage, the hum from some kind of utility reaching me, and retraced the way that Oona had come. There were no leaves or glass as I had thought there might be—she must have found another way in—but the Georgian-style glass looked out onto even more leaves and shards of wood than I had thought possible. To my right, multiple coverings half-tented what could only be a dining table and chairs to the side of the open room. The draped end of a covering had been spun into a circular bed and a few small chunks of bones exposed Oona's habits. At the other end, oak farmhouse cabinets formed a kitchen.

A deep breath escaped me. My urgency had fled. Standing at the porcelain sink, I didn't know what I'd expected to feel after so long. I had known I wouldn't find anyone waiting for me. I had known it would just be a house, albeit a house that might someday be a home again.

I looked around, hoping for some sense that I had been here before. Maybe Mum had just taken us to this town for a day-trip, rather than seeing my father again. It seemed like a shame that all those memories had turned to dust with her. The unbearable knowledge that I would never see her again clawed its way into my chest once again and refused to be extinguished. Unbidden, the mirthful light in her eye, wide descriptive expressions, and lilting tales stirred my memories. I would never get her back. I bit my tongue, the sharp immediacy breaking through the hot pressure in my throat and focused on the possibility of finding their secrets within those walls.

It was late winter, the light had reluctantly stayed a few more hours that day but hadn't yet convinced the warmth. I felt the difference in the air as I stepped outside, though I had only been in the house for a few moments. Dampness clung to the ground and a hue of grey tinted the street as I looked back towards the shops. I regretted not driving closer in that moment, knowing there was a perfectly reasonable parking excuse at the time. There were shops that would be sensible to check along the way too, so I felt my bag for the shape of my wallet.

The day the shadows had noticed me at Joanne's shop had left me with a lasting paranoia. I was young enough that, to this day, I doubted what I saw. Maybe I had doubted myself at the time too. I remembered checking my eyes as reaching fingers of devoid light had swept an icy awareness over me, it had left me nothing but dread and numbness. It had crawled after me when I'd slid from the stall to Mum serving a customer, it had reached into the shadow of the wall and undulated towards us. By the time I'd cried out, I was convinced there was more to this world and the need for something more dampened any effort to try that grew. The experience was my constant companion, but it had never happened again until that day I was walking back to Rosie.

At first, I thought I should've accepted Eoghan's cup of tea when the corners of my vision dimmed so minimally, it could have just been a dark cloud passing. Hairs shivered on the back of my neck and my eyes were drawn to the shadows that were lengthening too quickly for the passing of time.

My heart beat in my ears. Absolute truth and clarity seared against the pity and concern of the past— I had been right. My body moved on instinct, fearing its numbness. The only way to survive, away, away.

It billowed, the shadows around me growing denser, darker, devouring.

I looked down the street, only now noticing the emptiness of the shops. People had already set down their days and joined their families, protected from the threats. My stride widened, not caring for the odd jog that lunged from me.

"And the evening started out so nicely, didn't it?" A woman joined my stride, and I cried out in surprise. Her narrow face followed my turn back to the shadows, and she had to sweep her sleek orange hair away. "The weather, I meant, but that's no fun either."

Looking between her and the shadow, I noticed another woman and two men who hadn't been on the street a moment ago. With her back to us, the other woman stood closest to the darkness, only taking a step or two back for every five of mine. The men were side-on, mirroring my looks but doing so expectantly. It was still heading this way.

"You can see that?" I gasped. Tentative relief loosened my shoulders until I instinctively continued to rear back, knowing I wasn't safe if these people were running like I was.

"You could go so far as to say we were looking for it. If you have a car nearby, now's the time to drive away quickly."

"Do you?" I asked. "Where are you going to go?"

"We'll be fine, please run."

I hesitated for a moment longer, grappling with how they were going to be okay and just leaving them. I didn't want to feel that way again, drifting. So I ran. The rest of the street pounded beneath my everyday shoes until I could see Rosie sitting forlornly in the car park. I fumbled with my bag's familiar zip without glancing over my shoulder, trusting those four people. Schrödinger's strangers.

As I climbed into the driver's seat, the familiar surroundings began to placate the quaking in my limbs. Breaths heaved from me, and everything was quiet compared to the sound of my own blood. I just wanted to crawl into my back cabin, away, but instead I jammed my key into the ignition and drove.

• • • •

The following lunchtime, I found myself outside that now known house, ready to see what I could discover. I had not slept well in my insulated metal walls. For the first time in a long time, I had changed the batteries in the little LED lights strung to the ceiling and kept them on until dawn. I couldn't help but get up every time I got restless and check out the windows. I wondered what had happened to those people. There were no reports of anything strange in the morning that I could find. Would it happen again, or could I live another fragment of my life without it?

When I opened the door, I was faced with that delicate white snout again. I wasn't ready to talk more with Eoghan, so I pulled a slice of cheese out of my breakfast sandwich and greeted her with it.

"Hey, Oona, have you come to make good on your promise to help?"

She regarded me, softly accepted the cheese, and made a point of laying down with it in the hall.

"All right then, I won't hold it against you," I said, putting down the bags I'd carried in with me.

I thought my father's office would be the most interesting place to start; perhaps there would be details about the work that had taken up so much of his time or windows into his thoughts. It was possible that Mum had cleared the house after she'd received the news, but I wasn't sure when she would have done something like that.

I opened the brocade curtains and dust leapt into the air, caught by the midday sun. I folded the coverings with a little more care, trying not to send more dust floating. Musty books felt the warmth of light again, the memory of a smell lingered behind it. There were very few titles that I recognised. The ones I couldn't decipher looked like the script had come straight from another age. What language was this, and where would I find an expert to tell me what he'd been researching?

I wiped my hands, jeans freshly powdered, and slid one of the books from its place. The thin pages were sewn securely into a hardy well-made spine, it had clearly been used a lot, and the book fell into natural positions. Though a fine writing filled it throughout, there was often another hand underlining a sentence and adding its own notation in the margin. There were scattered drawings and diagrams too, sometimes a roughly-sketched landscape with defining rocks or cities, other times arrows gave a glimpse of their thought process. It could've been the notes that my father was studying, but there was a possibility that it was his handwriting. I wanted to run my fingers over the unknown language, some words looked familiar and I felt that it might be obvious with some references, but something sat heavy in my mind about finger oils and old books. It showed signs of wear but the pages were well looked after.

On other shelves, large amounts of the books had blank spines. Placing the one I held aside, I reached two shelves above to slide one of those free. The leather and bindings were surprisingly similar, the handwritten language inside was the same and more obviously my father's words. Its green ribbon admitted me to the last entry opposite a blank lined page. I perched on the edge of the sofa and continued turning the pages backwards. These pages weren't as soft as the last book, and columns of listed numbers gave it away as a kind of record— those low numbers couldn't possibly be dates, though. Eoghan's response about travel resonated with what I was seeing when I recognised some of the locations: the Hill of Tara, Greece, Tibet. Other entries were written in that strange, curved alphabet. Occasionally there were extra notes, and I spotted that when there was something in the last column, he recorded fewer trips that held the same date. Surely these couldn't all be his. Had he been recording the trips of other people too?

Muscles cramping, I straightened my back and swivelled my neck. Unseen from the doorway, I saw a tall, matching oak filing cabinet. Cup handles and wide fronts betrayed what the lock kept hidden. My curiosity mounted as I realised my father kept records safe in another language and also kept other bits of paperwork locked away. Had his travel been a front for something? It would've provided a reason for his and Mum's argument.

Distantly, I heard a bark and jumped. It sounded like Oona, except it could have been outside. Much of the street was hidden by overgrown shrubbery past those framed windows, but in the space overlooking the front wall, a man with dark, chin-length hair startled me. He passed for a second time, blocking the light momentarily as he pushed back his hair and shaded his eyes to peer around the house. It struck me that he could have been there last night, and nausea crept up my throat. I hadn't focused on the two men, and I barely remembered the women, but the shape of his jaw and his eyebrows seemed seared into my memory alongside the shadow. I moved suddenly, needing to talk to him. What had happened last night? But by the time I'd placed the book alongside the first and got up, he was gone.

I checked the hall to find Oona in the same place I'd left her, her eyes split briefly to acknowledge me. I listened for a moment longer before trying the filing drawer, but was unsurprised when it resisted. I was now familiar enough with the office's layout that the little drawers of the desk were the natural place I'd hide something like a key. The adrenalin that had kicked me up a minute ago turned to excitement, anticipation began to grow in my stomach and the interest of unearthing something dulled the little panic I had felt. There wasn't too much or too little that I wouldn't be happy to find out and I knew that even if it was a dead-end, there were still other places to look around the house.

I pulled on the little carved divot at the back of the desk. It was filled with keys of every style, and it felt like a deliberate joke. I stared at them, willing them to give up their secrets, before spilling them across the desk like water. So many of them were of heavy brass and iron that I wouldn't believe that they all still unlocked things. Among the ones with decorative spirals and curves forming their bodies, there were modern keys too, slim and cleanly cut. My hands rippled over them, flattening them into a single layer when there was a knock.

I looked up, thinking that whoever was at the door could be utterly normal and wanted to talk about religion or politics, but thought it more likely that whoever it was might give me more questions to find answers to. The keys whispered between themselves, and I felt tantalisingly close to unlocking something. I told myself to be quick. Oona had moved without me noticing, an alabaster figure sitting behind my shoulder, watching, head tilted. I hesitated, not knowing how she would react as I had little to judge her by. I felt like I was answering the door at Olivia's house.

As the two figures were revealed by the opening door, I felt the warmth drain from my hands.

Chapter
Four

"It's you! Look who it is, Drust. Surely that can't be a coincidence." The woman who had told me to run from the shadows looked back at me, her eyes wide with the same shock I felt. She nudged the man who stood behind her. The man with dark hair whom I had nearly gone after only moments ago. I couldn't see the other two from last night from where I was. Was this a coincidence? Had the shadows come alive to my father too?

"What was that? What happened? Is everyone okay?" Words fell out of my open mouth as if we had just come straight back here. The coldness left me clammy. "Is it here?"

Drust nudged the woman back in a purposefully theatrical manner. "Well, this is your area of expertise, I might take the day off," he said, beginning to turn until the woman held his arm.

She lowered her voice, though it wasn't difficult to make out her words. "Yes, but the Gwyn's hound is yours."

He looked up again, his tilt mirroring Oona's behind me.

"A what, sorry? Is that a breed?" I felt like I was seven years old again, asking questions about things deemed too adult for me to know.

"You know what?" the woman said suddenly, "I just found this great café, you might need a coffee if you want to know? I'll try to answer your questions if you try to answer mine. You should know that you're not completely safe but then, nobody is these days."

The choice brought me to the edge of something I didn't even know I was standing on. Was I willing to risk feeling that darkness again for some immediate knowledge about my father? Would I come across information without them anyway? I looked between them. Drust had raised his hand whilst the woman was speaking as if about to interrupt her. But now the question was out, he examined me directly, eyebrows drawn together, waiting.

The keys would still be beached on the side of the desk, I thought, but what Drust and the woman might know was worth the longer wait. I reached for my coat and met Oona's stare. "Be good."

Áine, the woman's name turned out to be, led us to what seemed like the closest café to the house. The bay windows exhibited a small but busy layer of tables before the counter. When the door opened, the smell of coffee was made lighter by the sweetness of the handmade cakes. I wondered if they had actually been here before or if that was simply a white lie to make me feel safer. Other conversations bubbled over us as she made her way to a corner table overlooking the street, inconspicuous.

"So," she began, "why don't we take it in turns to answer questions?"

I sat opposite her, the wooden chair curved around me. Drust made his way over to the small queue as if they had indeed been here before.

I nodded. I'd thought about this during our short walk—what I actually wanted to know from them and how much they were likely to know. "Okay... did you find me on purpose?"

Áine raised her chestnut eyebrows ever so slightly, a grin hovering in her expression. "It actually was a coincidence. Last night, we thought you were just in the wrong place at the wrong time, and we really hadn't been expecting you when we knocked. How did you know Peredur?"

His name seemed to make it real again; the things I wanted to know had a shape, and I needed something solid to hold on to. Up until this point, it was as if what I might find out was just a silhouette. I took a quiet breath.

"I didn't, really. I'm his daughter." We both tested the waters first.

"That might explain the coincidence away then," Drust said as he set down a tray of pots, milk, and sugar. A pot of tea and a pot of coffee. He poured the black coffee for himself. "The shadow creature recognises the part of you that's Peredur."

"Recognises?" I repeated, shaking my head slightly to Áine's offer of tea, the mint sharp in the air. "What is it? And what does it want? How did you get rid of it last night?"

"There are some things—" Drust started, before furrowing his brows when Áine interrupted him.

"Yes. We only have theories. And we didn't get rid of it."

Drust's focus bored straight towards her. "Áine! We should discuss how much she needs to know."

They silently quarrelled for a moment whilst I tried to work out how they might be involved, they knew each other well enough to row but there was an unspoken hierarchy that Drust tried to wield. His jaw tensed and he massaged his forehead as Áine turned back to me.

"The very bottom line is that we work for the same... community... that Peredur worked for, and we were sent to secure something from his house that belongs to us because whatever that shadow is has been taking others from us."

"Why now? As far as I'm aware, my dad's been gone five years or so."

Áine wrapped her hands around her cup. "Our resources have been cut somewhat recently. Your father's house wasn't a high priority until we detected a change."

"Was it me or that *thing*? And detected how?" Was there surveillance I should be worried about?

"Some things are not for us to talk about," Drust finished quietly, he took a sip of coffee. "How do you control the dog?"

I didn't understand the path that question went down and paused. It was a question that echoed his initial carefulness when he'd recognised her, but as Áine listened in, I couldn't help but think that Oona was involved in this too. Did that mean she was dangerous? Eoghan hadn't been concerned. Did that make Eoghan part of this as well?

"I haven't been here long, but she's been quite well-behaved, really. I only know that a neighbour's looked after her since my father passed."

"A neighbour?" I didn't miss their shared look.

"You might know him actually? Eoghan Wilkins, I think it was?" Their shared expressions revealed a touch of curiosity after their initial surprise.

"He lives on the same street. I walked the dog back, after finding her in the house the first time. He didn't mention that she'd been difficult either." I finally took the pot of coffee myself before adding milk and sugar to my cup. It seemed enough to fill the pause whilst Drust pulled out his phone and Áine decided how to respond.

"The dog's a particularly rare... breed and notoriously loyal. Perhaps through association with the house, she's retained some of the obedience she had with your father. We might need to talk to your neighbour too— he might be able to help us. But in the meanwhile, I want you to be careful and try not to do too much if the dog seems upset."

"She obviously wondered who I was at first but..." I shrugged. I'd begun to enjoy having her nearby. "Did you work with him? My father? I know he travelled around a lot." I didn't cast the question at either of them, but Áine didn't seem to mind answering. I wondered if being less direct with my questions helped.

Áine nodded, absently. "I only met him once, in passing. He was very busy at the time though and probably didn't even notice me." It roughly fit with what I'd already heard about his work, but some of the vibrancy had fled Áine's voice, and I knew there was more to it.

I glanced over to Drust, hoping he had pieces to give me as well, to find his gaze already on me. He was clearly reading me, watching for my responses as much as I was trying to gauge theirs. I didn't have anything to hide. I had to remind the hairs on the back of my neck that I was entitled to learn what I could, as his daughter. A stranger.

"My work crossed his path a little more. Your father was always helpful, where he could, and I've never heard anything but the utmost respect spoken about your family," he said finally in soft tones. "Have you found out much about his work?"

And just like that, I had to cede a small shake of my head. "Pieces," I said, and then thought that they might know someone who could read those strange, curved letters. I might have asked Áine about it nicely if we were alone, but it didn't escape me that it was likely written that way because of their community.

"I've only found some records at the house so far, but I couldn't read them. Some of them looked like research, if that's what belongs to you?"

"It might be useful. We've lost a lot recently, and it would probably help in rebuilding when we can." He hesitated and for a moment, I waited for him to continue.

"I understand that for some reason I can't know everything." I looked between them, invoking the fear I felt from my encounters with the darkness and the need to know what happened between my parents. Blood drummed in my right arm, resting on the table. "But I don't know what to think— I don't know what to do if those shadows come back. How am I supposed to move past this when I came here for answers? Am I even in danger? Who are you really?"

Áine turned to Drust whilst I was mid sentence, expectant; what they said next was obviously under his influence. Drust stared into his cup then ahead out the window before saying, "There are things we can't say. But for what we can, we'll want to look around your father's house. That's important too." He met my eyes, and his intensity stilled the fear and the need that I hadn't been able to calm. "Would you promise us that?"

I held his look, the cafe muffled beneath the beating in my ears, and nodded. I supposed it was only natural to start imagining what they needed from my father. When I'd been in danger, they'd helped me, and I thought that deserved some help in return. I didn't have anything to hide. And if it was beyond me, I could always drive away.

• • • •

Passing the ever more familiar gardens back, Áine perked up again and explained that we could have a proper conversation when we got in. By the time we had walked back over to the house, I was beginning to wonder what I had agreed to and if my time would have been better spent exploring on my own. They couldn't stop me searching at the same time as they did, though.

Oona hadn't moved from her curl in the garage doorway when I filed in with Áine behind me. Drust followed a moment later with the other man that had been there last night. She pricked her pink ears and opened her eyes at the same time wariness crept across my shoulders.

"There was one more of you, right?"

31

Áine nodded and gave me a reassuring smile. "Yes, Freda will keep an eye out for anything outside. This is Urien, he's been reporting what happened." She gestured towards the man with olive skin and smooth features.

I greeted him. They all had different roles to fill and I wondered what Drust had meant earlier about Áine's area of expertise. What did that make his area?

"Though watch this one." Áine smirked and nudged towards the newcomer. "I never know why he relays the messages, when we could all just be on speaker."

"You've got me." He acted as if he were hurt by her accusations. "I'm secretly diverting all our instructions."

Taking a step back into the study doorway, I took the opportunity to check the time and instead saw that Olivia had messaged.

Hope you're finding what you wanted to find. If it's too much right now, it will always wait until another time x

She was probing to see how I was feeling, like Mum used to, like I would automatically come apart at the first opportunity away. I didn't know if I was most annoyed at the lack of confidence in me or at how predictable I was. Taking a deep breath, I systematically checked the shadows, a new habit, whilst I ran through everything I'd discovered since my arrival.

This thing, my need to escape the shadows was linked to my father, whom Mum had moved us away from, whilst possibly knowing he may have been able to help. All of which may or may not be linked to this secretive community he worked for, whose documents were locked away and undecipherable, who were in opposition with these shadows and were somehow able to convince said shadows to leave.

Suddenly, it felt like the more I learnt about all this, whatever it was I was trying to work out got further and further away. I asked myself again why it was important. Last night had probably only happened because I'd driven here and there were still so many places I could experience. But at the same time, I knew I was staying because it had happened again. It validated a defining experience of my childhood. There really was more.

The keys caught my eye. They were still strewn across the leather writing pad of the desk. Examining the keyholes of the filing cabinet, I stretched my hand out and skimmed over their tide to find two similar brass designs.

"Hi there, girl, we're on Peredur's side." I peered into the hall and watched Drust offer his hand for Oona to smell, gaze averted, before turning back to try one of the keys. When nothing unlocked, I tried the same key in the bottom drawer. I had to look up again when a heavy thud trembled through the cup handle. Oona sat up but stoically stayed in her spot. Urien walked down the hall. Whilst I didn't trust them exactly, I didn't have any attachment to the house.

The drawer was full, files stacked all the way back, and only broken by little cardboard markers with those dates on them. I pulled one of them out and found what looked like an agreement, a waxy seal stamped in the middle of the page, handwritten words setting terms above accented signatures. Checking another couple told me they were all going to be the same. Had he been a part of some type of embassy? Who had he been making agreements for?

"Those were supposed to be protecting us, only they don't seem to be doing what they should be these days." Áine stood in the doorway and pointed to the papers in my hands. Then, before I could ask what they were for, she continued. "Drust's sure he can convince your dog that we're friends, so I wanted to check that all this is really okay?"

I nodded slowly, hardly registering her words and hardly concerned about what Oona's opinion of them might be. If they were worried about her, I might be able to use that to get away if I needed to. I echoed those same consolations to myself, brightening my expression to match hers. I could unravel more of this being here with them, than I could by myself. All it took was a stray word or absent thought and it might sate some of these questions. What had happened that made Mum think it was best for us to leave? They seemed to think the shadows reacted to my being here, and if that were the case, what if I couldn't escape it anyway?

"Her name is Oona," I said, nodding again towards her white form; the hallway guardian.

Áine's eyebrow bounced, and there was a laugh in her expression. "I'm not sure if that's supposed to be a compliment or an insult, but she's probably been named after one of our governors." She checked back on her colleagues for me and then said, "All this pretence must be irritating and I'm sorry. Though I want you to know that there won't be any going back if we tell you everything. This is a new situation for us too and we'll need to be able to explain our decisions at our briefing later."

"What's your area of expertise?" I asked suddenly, her words came too smoothly to be anything but a mediator.

"Diplomatic relations." She grinned. "I've worked with them all before, you might say Freda and I work for the same department. You've probably guessed Urien's communications.

And Drust is basically a type of field researcher... but I didn't call him that." She came in, sparing a glance towards the rest of my findings, the open books, and collapsed into part of the sofa that I'd bundled the sheets onto.

"These theories you have about that shadow... is this magic? Or supernatural?"

I wanted to believe her when her face grew serious. "Aren't they the same thing really? You can trust me... but I can't guarantee your safety. That would be careless when we don't know for certain what is going on. If you stay for the time being, we will try to keep you safe out of respect for what your father did."

I had to remind myself that people could train their mannerisms just as easily as they could train their words. "What did he do?"

Though she seemed to be sincere as she said, "He saved a lot of people."

"Miss Woods? Morgan?" Drust called. I quickly stashed the papers back in the drawer as he arrived at the doorway. Afterwards, I wondered if I'd been worried about them taking all my father's work, just when I was beginning to learn more. "Your father's hound—"

"Her name is Oona," Áine said, struggling to hold her face straight.

He looked between us both, verifying how serious she was being, until he muttered, "Well, I don't think Urien needs to report that ba—"

When a loud, deep rumbling echoed over to us, it was the same noise Oona had made when I'd first arrived. In the time it took me to look around, her growl mounted, and I knew immediately, from being the receiver of that threat, that something was here. I couldn't see her, and the hall was empty. Clouds dimmed the light from the windows and, all at once, everything went dark.

Chapter

Five

I plunged into ice. Eternity yawned before me, cold and unforgiving. There was no time left. The world ceased to exist, and everything was out of my reach. Perhaps it had never existed. I had wasted it.

But then the room and the windows flashed, Freda called to Áine and Drust from the doorway, in a lilting, accented language. Oona snarled somewhere; guttural noises that should have come from something far larger echoed around the room, chasing the shadows and growing louder and louder until I had to shield my ears. I followed the others to the hall, stumbling when the world briefly disappeared again.

Dense shadows, a devouring maw, converged on the door that Oona had been so intent to sit in front of. Dark undulations thumped where she had lain and against the frame, but light rippled throughout the shadow every time it struck. The walls lit up and I could see Oona's hackles magnified against the mass.

I froze, I couldn't shout. I didn't want it to notice me. The others might have shouted my name but when my eyes flicked their way, they were concentrating on the light outside, murmuring the occasional word to themselves. The need to move, to get away, overwhelmed me until it was painful. What did it want? I saw my life span across the darkness, my family's lives before me and our link throughout time.

But then something shifted and connected beyond the darkness. The absence of that wasted sensation washed over me. I would have been relieved, except as the thumping from the darkness ceased, it quickly became obvious that its attention had shifted.

The low snarls from Oona felt like a horrid backing track as the shadows became so heavy, it emerged like a fog only a short reach away. A void. Nothingness.

It struck and, whilst the shadows gripped me, my perception of how long we'd been there flickered. Had it been seconds or days? I struggled to breathe, until the hallway materialised again for longer than a heartbeat. In that moment of clarity, the light rippling from the door behind it surged. It was broke through the shadows, evaporating the fog, until I could no longer stand. Air was forced from my lungs, my head floated, and once again, the clouds seemed to slowly dim the light from the windows.

I was awake before I opened my eyes. A part of me was tired that all the same questions still mattered, but the bigger part of me was relieved that there was still time. I could still do something. Would I wish something so fragile away?

I could hear murmurs, the odd word— sometimes it might have been a different language again. It sounded like an argument about something. I moved my legs to find them raised off the end of something padded. I felt with my fingers to find the smooth, tough curve of the sofa in my father's office. Whatever had happened felt like a distant nightmare. In that moment, all I wanted to do was to avoid that feeling again, and I didn't know if it would keep happening whether I stayed on this path or not.

A delicate snuffle, followed by the cool wetness of Oona's nose, grazed the side of my head. The comfort of long-lost familiarity shivered down my neck, and I felt the corners of my mouth smile. The soft arc of her head butted my palm, her rigid ear yielding through my fingers. I received a swift lick to the back of my hand before I patted around to find only empty air.

When I heard footsteps heading in on the wooden floor, my eyes leapt open and my shoulders coiled, still running on impulse, not knowing what to expect until Áine was on her knees before me. She began saying soothing things and asking how I was. My memory reeled as it reminded me of how little I knew again. Would they tell me any more now? Did I even want to know anymore if the experiences would get worse?

"...you hear me? Can you tell me where you are?" I focused on her as the figures of two men and another woman rounded the door. Drust studied me as intently as Áine, eyebrows crooked in thought.

My throat felt as dry as soot when I croaked the hope circling my brain. "Is it gone? What happened?"

Áine swivelled her feet to one side and the others circled round a little more. Drust nearly sat with us.

"We were attacked," she said. "One of our protocols when securing these sites is to reinforce whatever protection there is at the time. I'm sorry but this time it was our fault. Your father seemed to have his own ways of doing things, and that dark creature must have sensed when there was a break in his old protections."

"Which is another reason why we should report in again," Urien mumbled distantly. The others exchanged looks before Drust turned and, nodding from Urien to the hallway, left me with Áine and Freda.

"I feel somewhat responsible, Miss. I should apologise." The other woman's accent was more rhythmic, and her features darker than everyone else. The seriousness in her apology preserved what she'd seen in her role as defence.

I could have just died. That was the situation. That feeling of loss wouldn't have even been a feeling if that had happened. It was just as ethereal to me as the belief that my father was related to all this. The shadows held more substance to me. Was continuing down this road the same as wishing my life away? I needed to think about this more before inevitability took hold like gravity.

Pivoting to feel less like the victim, I sat up slowly, blood rushing from my head.

"Are you feeling okay?" Áine half offered her arms as makeshift support, but I nodded.

"I'm fine." I tried what I hoped to be a supportive forehead crinkle when I looked back to Freda. "It's fine. I get the feeling things could have been worse if all of you weren't here anyway."

I glanced out the window and over the garden. Eoghan stood a short distance away between Drust and Urien, both hands resting on his walking stick. It was too far to make out the shape of their words, though I tried to read their moving lips, the occasional gestures implied it was about the attack.

"Eoghan worked for your community too, didn't he?"

Áine nodded. "He was a bit of a legend around the time we were getting into our work. None of us worked with him though."

Drust and Eoghan continued talking when Urien strayed away to make a call. By the time they came back in, Eoghan had left after sending a concerned look through the window. In the hour it took for a coffee to nurse me, Freda stationed herself back outside and Urien returned to brief Áine. When she came back in, she was alone and sat beside me on the sofa.

"So what do your higher-ups say about all this?"

She looked at me earnestly. "This mixture of events has led them to think revealing our nature should be the way forward." My heart began to quicken in anticipation, I stayed silent for fear of changing her mind. "You could start to understand all this in your own time anyway but, Morgan, I want you to be cautious when you make this decision."

I let my brain stew with this information, even though I knew I wouldn't come to any other decision, and nodded.

"Okay, well, we believe you are more your father's brethren than your mother's. We are the descendants of the Tuatha Dé Danann, the people of Danu, and work for the Seelie Council."

I recognised one of those words, and cast around in my mind for the others, processing the rest, "Seelie, like fey? What are you asking me to believe?"

"It is said that the Tuatha Dé Danann possessed certain skills." She inclined her head, perhaps deciding the best way to continue. "As a people, we are more attuned to the natural energies around us and, to a certain degree, can influence them too. We're at war, Morgan, and this dark creature is seemingly being used against us. We had to evacuate our city... well, tried to, so many were left behind... but when our gatekeepers didn't return, we couldn't afford to send more." She held my gaze meaningfully.

"Gatekeepers... like my father?"

"Yes. Gatekeepers inherit something rare, they are realm-walkers."

"That's enough, Áine." Urien appeared in the hallway and, as if breaking a spell, I had to look between them, force myself to see them.

I didn't know what to think. I had to get up, as if the cogs needed me to move. And for the first time since the attack, I left the house. I found myself walking the same route as before, the shop fronts' wide brickwork becoming as familiar as the stonework beneath my feet. I didn't even care that they were still at the house without me. I had been right. Life was more than it seemed, society as we knew it was a big ruse. Ironically, I would never feel sane again.

A figure walked towards me, a woman speaking on the phone. Cool air filled my lungs, moisture clung to the air and the breath shuddered in my throat. Mum had known— of course she had. Why else would we have moved? Did that make it worse that she hadn't told me after my experiences? Had my father wanted us to stay away for both our sakes?

In the untold coordination of passing by, I looked at the woman again only to notice the grey tinge of her skin. Her eyes flickered to mine as we passed— there was black in her eyes where there should have been white. As if locked by a magnet, my body turned to establish what I had seen. She kept going, obviously not caring for my reaction, and continued her conversation. I checked around, looking for someone else to tell me what I had just seen, and stumbled to a pause.

Almost instinctively, after not finding anyone immediately close by, my gaze darted to the areas of shadow. But they stayed where they were. I backed towards a bench overlooking a small park and sat. Was it the place, being so close to this gateway? Wouldn't people have heard about a place like this?

Past the entrance, the park path wound past a gentle hill and over a little bridge built for a man-made troll of chalk and fairy moss. Bunches of sunlit trumpets lined up along the hedges backing onto gardens from another street. A child squealed at the other end of the park and was chased over the patches of vibrant grass that had woken up to the spring music. That was the normality my parents had decided we wouldn't have. I'd come back to know if I'd have made the same decision. Would I be a different person if we'd stayed?

But now I was part of all this regardless of my parents' arrangement. It hadn't mattered. Would my choice now even have any significance? Despite the afternoon sun breaking through the remaining winter chill, the situation closed in around me, suffocating. My palms were clammy, and I hid my fingers in my sleeves to warm them.

I still wanted to explore and experience. I needed to know what the world offered before making this decision. And yet, I had chosen to come here first. I had deemed this important enough for me to put off other places. A small part of me was aware that by answering my curiosity, I had already sealed how I was going to live afterwards.

The child shouted again and darted around a group of teenagers, laughing. The mother went to follow, but one of the group stuck their bag out, and she tripped. I watched, social morality pushing me to speak out, but if anything went awry, I knew I had no way of actually helping. The culprit caught the mother's arm to stop her from falling. Her face opened up in relief, even as the colour drained from her face. Her movements were apologetic and thankful whilst the skin around her eyes darkened. She wiped her brow, as if she'd suddenly grown feverish.

Another in the group looked my way, its nose and ears flat, predatory. I looked to the mother again who laughed and called to her child, taking them under her protection and displaying affection all at once. And then they walked away, the child babbling loud enough that I could still hear an occasional intonation. They gave me no reason to believe they were seeing what I was seeing. I looked straight back over to the group, as if it would answer what they had just done. They were laughing, one of them pointing at another. The one who had spotted me didn't look back. My head pulsed after witnessing *something*. The group had pried fun from her health, but obviously cared as much for my reaction as the woman on the phone. The woman and child were still walking— they hadn't taken her life, but she looked like she might need to rest with some lemon and honey for a few days.

After I couldn't see the woman anymore, I turned. I didn't want to know what had happened. Maybe she just had a low immune system. Maybe this didn't have to involve me. I headed frantically towards Rosie. How far I might be able to get away from all this? I was happy to come back and see what was left after these people were done. I still had my key, I reminded myself as I focused on the pavement, and if they changed the locks to the house... so be it. I still hadn't moved anything of mine so I began to think that I could probably drive off without them noticing. It would probably be a relief for them anyway.

The moment I could see Rosie's end, my stomach clenched, as if I was only normal when my escape wasn't in sight. I tried to speed up, but I didn't want to attract attention from the house. I didn't move my head in any discernible way. I could get in my van. I could drive away. I could still exist outside of all this for the time being.

A familiar calm blanketed me as soon as I closed the van door. I released the deep breath and waited just another moment before pulling my seatbelt over me. I hadn't planned where I was going to go. I'd done that before, driven to see where the road would go. If I stayed on this bit of land, I could always find my way back. I turned the engine on and the second I was about to drive off, the passenger door opened.

Drust leant in, his bomber jacket falling open. "It's not my intention to stop you, don't worry. It would probably make things simpler even but... Can I have a second?"

I eyed him, knowing whatever he wanted to say was to try and convince me of something, regardless of what he'd just said. But I found myself thinking that if it had been Áine, Freda, or Urien, I wouldn't have been as curious about what they had to say. I gave a small nod, turning the engine off, before he sat on one knee and pulled the door closed after him.

"Since you connected with your father's gift, I think it'll be unlikely the world will be the same for you again." He watched me from under a stray lock of hair, but I was unable to meet his eye. "But you've already found that out, haven't you? What happened?"

It didn't seem like something I knew how to talk about, a woman tripped— what was strange about that? I felt my focus shift through the windscreen, and I shrugged whilst I tried to think of the words. "I don't even know. It's me then? It'll be the same wherever I go?"

He lowered his gaze and tilted his head. "Probably, we've only recently begun to explore how others recognise this energy. In your case, I found it strange that both that dark creature and your father's hound were interested in you, so I think it likely that this was lying dormant in you until your family's gate was threatened."

I couldn't go anywhere. I had sealed who I was by coming here in the first place. My heart grew just as dense as the shadows I wanted to escape and sunk. The disappointment and anger clung to me, tightening my jaw, even as my eyes closed briefly into the last escape I had.

"We're going to work this out," he continued. "This impacts more people than you realise and we all want the same thing. There are those who live apart from all this though, your neighbour Eoghan has for many years out of necessity. It would be irresponsible of me not to mention that the Unseelie will find you an easier target if you do leave though, if you don't have a way to protect yourself."

Memories of Mum's last days were roused unbidden, provoked by what had happened in the park; the prominence of her once fine cheekbones and forehead displayed her strength in the face of her ongoing battle. Had she felt the touch of some darker force too? Had we been game as soon as we'd left my father? Should I have been able to protect her?

"I came here thinking I wanted to unravel these secrets," I said quietly, resting my head on the seat behind me. "It doesn't make sense why Mum kept this from me. I don't know what I was expecting— definitely not this."

He slowly shrugged, watching someone cross the road. "Would you rather not know, looking back? What I know about my family keeps me searching for answers. It's part of me now."

I followed the same person he did briefly, they carried shopping, the bold colours of branded boxes pressed up against the stretching plastic. "If I knew it was going to change me, I would've wanted a little more time. I think I still would have come here eventually."

"Then what's the difference?" He looked back to me. "Everything changes us, but we find ways to live with it anyway."

There was a story there. Of course, I wasn't so naive to think that everyone else's lives were unmarked, but I was interested enough in this little group, in this calm, solid presence next to me, that I wanted to hear about his life.

"What did your family do?" I met his look, hoping to shake him as much as his last observation had jarred me with its honesty. It really didn't matter when I'd come here, if I knew I would have come here in every situation.

He didn't answer immediately. One moment I thought he might leave me and Rosie to work out what we were doing but then he said, "My whole life would have been different if I hadn't been reclaimed, but the knowledge that it could have been a real possibility acts as my guide. I know that who I am now is decidedly stronger in that knowledge."

Would I get to the point where I was stronger because no one had been there to teach me? Was I capable of holding a truth as closely as Drust did? It obviously brought him confidence. I found the word reclaimed curious but didn't poke further. What society was I actually involving myself with? Who would oppose the shadows?

"Can you teach me how to be safe?"

"You'll probably pick some things up. We'll need to hear from the council before we do anything more with you anyway."

Chapter
Six

"Morgan?" Áine's voice came from the front door after hearing it open. Oona didn't even flick an ear, knowing full well when we were in danger. She remained in her den, shaped by her circling, not far from where I was at the kitchen table. Though I'd decided to stay and had seen them every day since, the group weren't staying at the house and usually left by the evening. When I was exploring the town, I often saw at least one of them around too.

They seemed particularly interested in the door I had assumed led to the garage, the same one the light had come from the day the shadow attacked. I hadn't tried to open it yet but none of them had stopped me examining my father's books in the meanwhile either. He hadn't lacked possessions, and I found that the homely features in each room were far more than a lifetime's collection of antique furniture. The furniture had been handcrafted and carefully looked after, delicately created porcelain hidden away behind glass, looking down upon me, faded photo frames on the sides and forgotten letters in piles on tables. Though the more frequented rooms had been reasonably well kept, the other spaces around the bedroom, kitchen, and office held boxes of even older clothes, books, and even weapons. Eoghan said that they'd been my grandfather's— what else used to belong to other members of my family here?

"In the kitchen," I said louder than usual. I made no attempt to move the photo albums and letters I had been studying on the table. Urien may have eyed them before, implying the importance of reporting whatever was found, but Áine had been quick to shush him. When she spoke about their way of governing and running their little group, I wondered if our systems seemed as fragmentary. Although everyone who associated with the court reported to the Seelie Council, smaller communities ran themselves where only the basics like food, shelter, defence, and Pacts were managed in the city, Falias. By the sounds of it, the council members who oversaw these main areas directed their recent evacuation. There was a noble family, who always had a member in the council, though Drust said they acted more like a figurehead now.

It was the council we had been waiting to hear from.

"They've arrived." Before she noticed what was laid out in front of me, Áine appeared in the hallway. She walked over and stood at my shoulder to have a look.

"All of them?" I asked.

"Oh... no, my darling, most of them stay at camp for their own safety, but Belenus, Master of Accords, and Agrona, Master of Alliance, would like to meet you before settling their decision." She tilted one of the letters her way, one of the ones I couldn't read, written in that curving, embellished language. I recognised the letters now but still had no point of reference. In whispered tones, Áine had given me the essence of some of the records one afternoon; descriptions of places travelled and who had gone with him. Only Drust had walked in, looked at us with equal scrutiny, before striding right back out the way he'd come.

"Can Eoghan be there?" From what I'd gathered, he'd been outside the Seelie circle for some time, and I hoped he would tell me if they were hiding anything. I felt like he might act in my father's best interests, but I didn't know if my father's interests lined up with my own.

Áine continued reading for a moment longer before looking back to me, a tilt in her expression, "We can ask... but when Mr Wilkins left, there was some controversy. Honestly, I was surprised he'd been living so close to the gate, but unfortunately that might work against him too."

"Wouldn't it only be fair to at least let him know what's going on?"

She nodded. "He knows. Agrona said he'd contacted them as well. From what I heard, it was more out of concern for you. Urien said he wanted to know what they were going to do to protect you." Then, tapping the letter still laid next to her outreached hand, she lowered her tone into mischief. "This is cute. Your father was writing love notes to your mother, this must be one of his drafts."

She didn't realise the impact her last comment had on me as she curiously lifted one bit of paper and then another. In a small gesture of friendly sharing, I suddenly knew my father was on my side, and his concern came through Eoghan, just like his love was recorded in his handwriting here. My father still cared for my mother, and he'd wanted to keep us safe. All at once, I felt his personality in the house around me and in his words before me. His presence echoed through his relationship with Eoghan.

"I might ask him anyway"—I swallowed and shrugged in an exaggerated gesture—"How am I supposed to know what your customs are?"

• • • •

When Eoghan and I joined the group at the kitchen table, Áine broke the silence by introducing me to the council members. Closest to the hall sat a stern-looking woman, unruly wisps of grey escaped the bun her coarse hair was pulled into. The lines around her black eyes revealed the depth of either the anger or laughter she'd felt throughout her life. Further in, a man with tawny skin wrote a few notes whilst they addressed the other man leaning on his stick. Eoghan reclined against the door to the garden, but he looked almost as uneasy as I was.

"Eoghan is a friend, and I'd prefer to have him here to support me." I leant on the nearby worktop, Áine stood on the other side of the peninsular, Drust and the rest of the group were at the table with our guests. Oona appeared to support my decision and padded from her spot in the hallway to stand in the doorway too. The note-taker smiled gently, his hooded eyes crinkling, whilst the woman raised an eyebrow. I wondered if they would be just as divided on other decisions and if that was why they were here.

The one who'd smiled, nodded, "This is your home. As far as I'm aware, the terms of Mr Wilkins' Pact prevented his return to Falias only. You look well, Eoghan."

"Belenus," Eoghan replied, tilting his head. "I was sorry to hear about the situation T'sol imposed on the good people of Falias."

The other council member interjected. I assumed she was Agrona. "I'm afraid the council hasn't even begun to discuss how this affects your Pact, Eoghan, though we cannot yet say for certain who's involved. Something must have corrupted him."

"I understand, friends. I'd be quite happy to live the rest of my days here. Regardless, I believe we're here to discuss the situation the Unseelie have put Miss Woods in."

"Quite right," Belenus said as he looked back to me curiously. There was no malice in his tone. "We understand you've had experiences with the shadow that's attacking our gates. Have you always had the sight?"

I wondered suddenly if I would have been more comfortable on my own. Childhood memories crawled down my spine, memories that I wished would stay buried, memories that made me shiver. I looked to Eoghan and Oona, then looked back, attempting to steel my expression.

"No, I haven't seen other creatures for what they were until recently."

Áine tilted towards me in an advisory manner and quickly whispered, "The term race is more acceptable."

"Our people are not animals," Agrona said, her posture just as tense as mine.

My face felt hot and cold at the same time, caught between regret and shame. I stood a little firmer, willing my nerve not to abandon me. "I meant no offence. I'm sorry— race. I'm still learning, and this is all still new to me." Then, swallowing, careful with the words I chose next, I said, "But I've seen the shadow before, though it never chased me like it did with Áine and Drust and the others."

The group's focus went from Belenus to Agrona to me. Drust's expression walled off again, focusing on me like he had in the cafe, eyebrows furrowed.

Urien quickly said, "Masters, I would have assuredly passed this information along had we been aware."

I nearly retreated to Áine again, fearing that I'd made another misstep when Drust spoke above Urien's muttering. "How long ago was that?"

Belenus raised his hand slightly to Urien as their attention turned back to me. It occurred to me that I could try to look as if I was thinking about it, but it was seared into my pathways. "Nearly fifteen years ago."

They looked to each other again, and something passed around the kitchen.

"What does that mean?" I followed their glances until Áine asked from behind me.

"Decision to let this poor girl in on what we know, please?"

The council members considered each of us. Belenus spoke first. "If she supports us, she'll learn eventually anyway."

"And if she supports them, we know she isn't bringing them any new information." Agrona nodded. "Continue."

I turned, resting my arm on the worktop between us. I could feel my blood dance against the chill surface, how could there be more to learn? My neck prickled with everyone's attention.

"There are other realms, like I mentioned before. The gates, like the one your family keeps, are a means to these places. Due to its position in relation to yours, the time in our world normally appears slower in comparison to this world. From our world, your lives pass very quickly— nearly seven times faster. Does that make sense?"

I tried to connect the fragments I'd collected. "So... what happened just over two years ago in your world?"

Her eyes flicked back to the others behind me briefly, as if checking her permission hadn't been revoked. "It could all just be a coincidence, remember, but... it's about the time a member of our prime family was murdered. It was devastating to our whole city. It meant the Unseelie were declaring war. And now maybe that's a little more proof that there's a larger plan."

I couldn't help but feel ignorant, unknowing, about how many people were suffering beyond my scope. Was this a cause that I could forgive my father for? "That's why you had to evacuate."

She nodded. "Many sought refuge then. The Unseelie seized a lot of towns at the same time but we stood at Falias, the prime daughters have been strong. When T'sol, their brother, claimed an authoritarian position about a month ago, the Unseelie rose up again. The lucky among us were able to seek shelter in some ancient refuge camps, we joined those who fled first."

Agrona tapped her bony fingers, turning to Drust. "What does this actually mean? How is the death of the prime father implicated?"

His normally stoic composure dropped just a second, uncertain, before Eoghan cleared his throat. "There is wisdom that says a terrible act releases its own darkness, though I'm sure we never recognised it would be so literal."

"Whatever it is"—Drust picked up, glancing at me—"its interest is in the old power: the gates, the gatekeepers. If T'sol's actions created this shadow, this may have all been planned. Why is it only attacking now?"

"And what do the Unseelie want with that energy?" Freda said.

"If I have this ancient, mystical gift," I said, "why wouldn't they take it from me when I was younger?"

"It's not that black and white." Drust shook his head. "I'll bet you've never had the reaction you had when it attacked the house here either? Your connection with the gates goes back through your blood to the very first keepers. Our people were driven out of this world, and the connection your family wields is part of what saved us." I saw his focus shift inward as his ideas took priority. "What's strange... is the strength of your connection despite your heritage. There might be a possibility that you have someone quite powerful on your mother's side too."

A side of me recognised how little I knew about my lineage, whilst the other turned away. I glanced around the group, but they only waited, half expecting me to know who he meant.

"I think one family mystery at a time is enough," I mumbled.

Eoghan cleared his throat and, likely aware of how I felt about the secrets that I was only just discovering, turned the focus back to the matter at hand. "The Unseelie can do a lot if they have a supply of old energy. I am aware this could be sensitive too, but are we allowed to know what else happened? Two full council members meeting a dormant gatekeeper... Falias was defensible. Something else happened, didn't it?"

Agrona and Belenus looked at each other, I wondered if there were certain topics they had discussed before coming. Had the council met before they left to meet me?

Belenus rested back, balancing his gaze between Eoghan and me, "By all accounts of those who managed to cross back over, the time rift closed behind them, travel between realms is no longer possible. Reports say it was approximately one to two weeks ago, which lines up with the attacks." I watched as Agrona studied Eoghan, it seemed like if she never saw him again, it would have been too soon. His furrowed brow deepened, accompanying the murmur that echoed around the kitchen; I would have been convinced if I had been the one suspicious of him.

"They could be evening the advantages?" Freda interrupted the pause, her body tilted in the direction of the door, like Oona when she didn't fully settle. "They'd be aware that the Seelie, as a court, would have more time to plan their counter on this world?"

Belenus nodded slowly when Drust added, "But how? We haven't been able to do something like that for generations."

In raising his palm a fraction, Eoghan dispersed whatever suspicion Agrona was nursing. "You might have to entertain the possibility that the Unseelie have part of the Stone of Fál."

I watched as tension darted between Freda and Urien, I heard Áine inhale behind me. I felt like the rapt audience, even while the rock in my stomach reminded me that this was happening to people they knew. "When the original gatekeepers split our world off, that was what they used— that stone could change our fate."

I was only just wading through what I'd understood when Agrona ended the discussion. Leaning forward, she must've thought it was important enough to end Eoghan's idea there as she said, "These ideas would be best discussed with the rest of the council, I think. Whilst I'm sure Miss Woods could benefit from building her knowledge, there is a risk that the shadow's interest in her could lead it back to our camp." Drust caught my look with his own, I hoped for any other little comment and more insight. He raised an eyebrow when I didn't trust myself to say anything as I waited. I could be left to the wolves just as easily as I'd given away my ignorance.

"On the contrary," Belenus responded, "if the shadow, and by extension the Unseelie, are interested in her, it would be in our interests to protect her as much as we can."

"Another point, Masters, if you'll permit me?" Drust said. "With her, we also might have a chance to learn more about what the Unseelie are planning by how they react."

"And how would we know what is normal and what is different?" Agrona barked. I was surprised at her venom, but Drust ignored it, even as his jaw tightened.

"The shadow might attack this area less too," Áine said abruptly, "and it only seems logical that it would be more persistent if it's after both Morgan and the gate."

Eyes no longer conversed across the room, and everyone waited for Agrona's acceptance. "Fine," she finally muttered. "Urien? Arrange a backup team to secure this site. Áine and Drust can escort Miss Woods if they're so sure about her. Freda, hold the area with Urien until support arrives."

The council members didn't stay long after a decision had been made. I watched as Urien and Áine waited to speak to them, heading into different corners of the house. Drust looked at me again from the table, and I suddenly wasn't sure what had been agreed upon. A sour taste crept up the back of my throat as if the shadows had found their way in without me noticing.

"Morgan?" Eoghan said from the doorway. I pushed away from the counter, attempting to remain casual to the raised eyebrow that I knew watched from the table, and followed towards my father's study where Eoghan stood. Oona was already back in front of the door that led to the gate, primly resting her head on her front paws. Her eyes flicked between us and the rest of the group.

"I know it's probably difficult to know what to do," Eoghan's voice was gravelly with concern, "but there are things to be aware of with the Seelie as well as the Unseelie. They may have lost their records for the time being, but their society still runs on agreements and Pacts. I want you to be aware of the full details if you're asked to agree to anything." I knew he only meant to prepare me, however the depth of what I didn't know yawned beneath me. Their ways were utterly new. I had hoped the truth that I'd come looking for would prepare me further for a life I wanted, instead, I felt like I had simply jumped from one set of jaws to another.

"Eoghan, how am I supposed to help? What are they going to want me to do? I don't know anything about all this." My throat began to close as he lowered his voice further.

"As far as I'm aware, neither do they. They've been forced into an awful situation. The son of the prime family was corrupted a long time ago, and the Unseelie are obviously manoeuvring. When I left after his turn, they thought I was involved too, but it's been long enough for me to know they only acted on the information they had at the time. What's odd is that, historically, there's normally far longer between wars. The prime son's turning must have rallied them together much quicker." He looked older than he had when we'd first met, the bags under his eyes darker. "They'll be trying to work out their next steps to take back their city, their heritage, but they can't do that without knowing what the Unseelie are planning."

"And I'm part of what the Unseelie are planning?" I didn't recognise my voice.

"They have found a way to summon this dark Aspect, so it must be in their interests to do so. The question now is what they want with the type of energy you can harness. You will be looked after with the Seelie, they'll prepare you, but you are involving yourself. You will have chosen who to follow, as it were." He waited for my response but all I could think about was how different it was to anything I'd expected. I was reminded of Drust's question and as I remembered the moment, my heart stuttered. Even if I had waited, if I would have still come seeking, what difference did it make?

"This is what killed him, Morgan. Your father? In amongst all this, your father was helping with the evacuations and one day... just didn't come back. I often wonder how many lives he was able to save. It was an honour to have known him, really, to be able to call him a friend." His tone was filled with the same warmth his look had.

I stared at an old photo of Mum and me that was on the desk. "Was all this the real reason Mum left with me?"

He shrugged slowly, "I can't say for certain, but I suspect so. The Unseelie had a major setback just before all this started, it made sense that they were going to take action again soon, and your father knew that. You learn to keep tabs on things like that, even being courtless."

I heard him respond but it felt like I wasn't registering anything he was saying. I had come this far already though.

"I understand," I said. "I was the one who came looking, I want to know."

Chapter

Seven

"**I**'m driving," Drust said, when we made our way towards my van a day after the council had left.

"I'm sorry, did I interrupt when you were having your moment?" Áine nudged ahead of him with her elbow. "Who knows where we'd end up if I let you drive. Leave these human things to me."

I was only a step behind them, still expecting to drive my own vehicle. Amused, I held the keys up obviously for them to see.

"Relax! We'll take it—"

"And where would you drive us—"

They said together after turning back to me. I smirked as Drust held out his hand expectantly. They raised a good point, I had no idea where their camp was, though they led me to believe we could drive there.

I threw the jangling set of keys, my means back to Olivia and Joanne, to Áine and said, "Fine. But you're paying for the fuel."

Drust headed around to the passenger's side the moment Áine whooped in his direction. I looked back towards the house once more, seeing it in its ordinary wonder for all the extraordinary that lay beneath, the natural in its supernatural. I walked these pavements with the same unsettled feet that had walked by the shore, and for the first time, I wondered if I'd expected to feel more at home here.

Oona's white figure emerged from the shadows by the house, and she sat on the path by the front door. Drust admitted shortly before we left that he'd been surprised to see one of her breed; there were only so many of them, no more, no less. He'd said, it made sense, considering the five years or so since my father had died, why securing it had been relatively easy. As Oona inclined her head before I got in, I felt lighter knowing she was protecting my father's house, along with Freda and Urien.

It was getting dark by the time we set off, heading north. Sitting in the back, I'd pulled back the kitchenette curtain to watch the directions Áine drove, but once we'd passed the last of the homely lights, the nighttime road consumed us. Drust was mostly out of my view from the backseat, where he was partly leaning on the passenger door. I could see the corner of the creased map I kept in the side propped up on his knee.

"Remind me whose good idea it was to travel at night?" I asked through the window, only seeing glimpses of other cars and roadside bushes in the headlights.

Áine smiled, casting a look briefly towards Drust, before answering herself. "It's actually not as bad an idea as it seems. There aren't many races that have an advantage in the dark, even among the Unseelie."

"What about the shadow?"

"It shouldn't be able to be everywhere at once," Drust said from around the corner, "even when we're surrounded by darkness."

I hoped I could trust what they told me, "Isn't that just theory though? Do you actually know what it is?"

He regarded me in the reflection of the window with eyes like stone. "Well, look at it this way, I have more experience in these energies than Áine has in human cultures, and you seem to trust her."

"Was that supposed to hurt?" Áine retorted. "Drust, love, you're supposed to be convincing her."

"Based on the pattern of its appearances, as well as its general movement, it appears to use the absence of light like a well-used path, the path of least resistance. It wouldn't go in a consistent direction otherwise, but appear from spot to spot."

Áine looked back to me through the rearview mirror and smirked.

"It also didn't act tireless," he continued, either plainly ignoring Áine or not caring he'd been provoked. "The times that Freda could relax showed us that *it*, or the it summoning it, burns out. But also, perhaps, that there are other things that take up their time."

It was cooling on that stone, in his gaze. Everything realigned as I thought about what he was saying. The streetlights flashed in front of us before we hit another stretch of winding country lanes. It was now completely dark ahead of the dusty cast of insects in the high beams.

"How long do you think it'll take to find us?" He looked away and I had to pull my jacket further around me.

"It's impossible to know whether it was drawn to you or your father's gate first," he said, "so I wouldn't like to guess. But whatever else it does, it left a couple of days in between where you weren't its focus. I hope that might be a guide of some kind."

"What would've happened if we'd used the gate?"

"To go where? The Unseelie would know where we were headed before we even arrived there. If they have access to even one gate, they can work out which other gates are drawing energy. We don't take our own safety any more lightly because we have you with us, we've thought this through."

· · · ·

By the time Áine indicated into a rest stop, I had been lulled into a monotonous rhythm. I'd dozed off a couple of times until three hours had passed, and it was well and truly night. I knew the country was only so vast though, and the unrecognisable arrangement of letters on a roadside sign gave away that we'd passed into Wales.

"I suppose you're not allowed to say where we're headed?" I muttered to Áine as we staggered from my van, stretching legs that had rested too long in one position.

"Well, in all honesty, it won't really matter by the time we arrive. When we head underground, it'll take a couple of days to settle in anyway."

"Wait, underground?" That was a detail Eoghan had forgotten to mention. Or maybe he really hadn't known where their evacuation camp had been. In that detail, there was less freedom than I'd hoped to have, but I was curious too. How had thousands of them survived by doing that? Where did that leave them if they were still trying to save people?

I followed them into the garishly bright cluster of restaurants and last-minute present shops. Mesh boxes of balls with cartoon faces sat like great rocks on the path leading to the toilets. Lone travellers rested at a safe distance away from one another, one face dissolving into obscurity before the next. In a café, a sallow pale-green face looked up from his newspaper. Black, half-moon glasses perched on the end of his bulbous nose, above two small tusks that poked out from his mouth. Like the others I'd seen by then, I told myself not to think of the preformed ideas I'd been given about orcs and trolls and discreetly looked again. He nodded in our direction and lifted his top lip, revealing some extra wide incisors, in what I could only discern as a smile. Looking to Áine for direction, I hoped to avoid agreeing to some kind of duel, or something I couldn't apologise away, when she'd already disappeared into the smells of toilet cleaner and the sounds of hand-dryers.

"You grabbing a sandwich or something?" I asked as Áine and I exited, relieved and refreshed. My eyes wandered back over the café, the small deli and souvenir shop to find more of the tables clear. The odd ceramic coffee cup had been abandoned and yet to be cleared. I waited for Drust, who leant between two shops with a hand relaxed in his pocket, talking to someone a few paces away. We must've still been okay timewise to find a snack.

"Maybe some crisps. I get odd looks when I try frying potatoes like that at home." She stumbled on the word 'home', before committing to say it properly as if she didn't want to replace where home was. My heart grew heavier, I wanted to comfort her like she had with me but any words my mind gave me didn't seem enough. I rested my hand lightly on her arm, hoping my friendship and support came across in such a small gesture.

"Why don't I get a little selection? Road snacks? I don't want you to try and pay with a fake fifty-pound note or however you're getting by."

She smiled lightly and held out Rosie's keys, "Thank you. Let yourself back in whilst I find out if this is work related?" She nodded over in the direction where Drust stood, and this time I noticed that there was a subtle transparency to the person he stood opposite. I thought about the flow of energy that had come to me when the gate was attacked and whether it had now worn such a distinct path, perhaps I would never be rid of it. This stream, these abilities I paddled in, I didn't understand how I'd been so blind before when I hadn't seen these people.

I headed back to my van with arms laden with colourful yellow, red, and blue logos. Out of the hundreds of miles I'd driven in my life, this was an area I hadn't yet been to, even though the sign layouts and road arrangements looked like any other. I could hear the nearby dual carriageway and the hum of engines that never slept. I pulled open the passenger-side door and let the supplies fall from my arms into the seat. Shamefully for the first time, the extent of what the Seelie had lost seeped over me; those who'd run might not ever know what happened to their friends and family. Who else hadn't made it to safety? I remembered Eoghan's situation and reminded myself that others had lost things because of the Seelie too. I had no way of checking the truth about what I was being told.

As I turned to see if Áine and Drust were on their way, something on the dashboard reflected the light from the service station. It was dull and brassy, the light coagulated and left blackened edges behind. It was a key, not unlike the ones I'd found in my father's desk, decorative spirals formed its head, and it had a baluster-style spine. The teeth were square and evenly spaced. What light there was seemed to be drawn into it, absorbed. Was this one of my father's?

It was in my hand before I knew what I was doing. I grabbed a bag of cheesy corn puffs and a caramel chocolate bar, then opened the back and retook my seat. The key rested cold in my hand as the other two jumped into the same seats only a few minutes later. I didn't understand why I'd done it, and I wondered whether I should say something; they had obviously needed it for something. I held it under my other arm. It was slightly oily. Whatever it was used for, it could have been used recently. I could smell the metal from where it was and felt grease smear over my fingers.

"Poor chap, got separated from his family. Getting more and more of those unfortunately."

And then the moment had passed a little too long ago. I could just say I'd forgotten to mention grabbing it for safe-keeping.

I rested back. Rosie had been one of my first projects after Mum died. I wanted to find a way to make it work, for the opportunity of discovering new places without contracting my life away, to be as free as anyone could be in this world. In that minute, we made our way back onto the road as a stray lamppost guided us over a roundabout. The situation I headed into made me think that maybe there could be other ways to be free. Whilst the metal in my hand warmed, my eyes followed a trail of my own whispering, sentimental things around the steel shell and inbuilt cabinets that felt more like home to me than anywhere else. The first scarf Olivia had been proud of knitting, a stone from the beach where I had first realised the enormity of the entity we lived on, the scrapbook I'd made of the photos and letters from Mum. Above all, I knew that if I had to seek further for other ways to be free, I would be the same person without these things I'd often held.

But could I give them up only to find the same systems? Or worse? I began to feel my hope spoil, leaving behind the acidic taste of fear and doubt. Drawing my knees into my chest against the darkness, I reminded myself that Áine would give me Rosie's keys back when we'd arrived. Out of the two of them, she would undoubtedly let me leave if I wasn't ready.

• • • •

The next time we stretched our legs again was in a dirt-tracked car park. We were the only vehicle I'd seen since the monotonous rhythm returned, but the final road had been so overgrown, I'd nearly had to make a case for Rosie's exterior. I looked around after jumping out, my hand sliding into my jean pocket to hold the cold metal key briefly. After I'd grabbed my camping backpack, I heard Drust's door, and a moment later Áine turned the engine off. She left the headlights on briefly, white light illuminating a path of trodden grass where it gradually got rockier. Off to the side, an even narrower lane found its way back down the cliff. But even with help from moon, the brightness didn't seep more than a few trees into the woodland around us.

Gravel shifted underfoot behind me in two steps. I was aware of Drust there, a subtle pressure where his presence made me conscious of my hands and the breaths I took. The dark pressed in on us like it had the night we'd been attacked, but as soon as I turned, he said, "Give me a moment," before treading carefully through the rocky grass. By the time Áine jumped out, he was out of sight, dissolved into darkness. Inexplicably, the absence of his presence left behind bittersweet relief and loss.

"Where's he gone now? What's wrong with using a torch like a normal person?" Áine tutted and reached into the backpack she had with her. It wasn't the first time I wondered what I was doing there, but even as I closed the sliding door, I remembered that there was no escaping it now. I felt a spike of apprehension as she dropped my keys into her bag after grabbing a torch.

"Áine? Could I keep the keys?"

She dipped her hand in again, handed them over and smiled. "Of course."

She indicated to the trees, and we began walking the direction Drust had gone, when there was a distant flickering of light. With every step we took, another white flame moved towards us, back to the van. I looked to her to see if we should be concerned.

"He's only doing this because you're here," she said, a knowing lightness dancing around her eyes. I was still trying to work out what was coming towards us when the sound of laughter arose and passed us.

Amongst the trees, curving lithe limbs jumped from branch to branch, their features lit from the glowing trail and were as pointed as the leaves that adorned them. They kept their distance, but Áine waved before she continued the same way. I heard rustling after the laughter faded and didn't think anymore of it when the droplet-like flames revealed Drust standing next to a more mountainous track. Shining green ferns poked their heads out of the ground all around us, and the guiding lights danced on their spirals. An owl called from a distant tree.

"I guess this way of lighting the woods is a little more befitting," I whispered to Áine. We began walking again, and I thought I saw Drust smirk as I turned.

"Please don't hate me for my ignorance," I said, certain that Agrona might have, as I checked the trees for the nymph-like women we'd just seen, "but the different races I've seen around... what are they?"

"So," Áine replied, making her way over, "many of the stories you might have heard divide our people into different species: elves, gnomes, goblins, mermaids, even." Drust made a noise not unlike a snort. "Similar tales around the world give them different names but, generally, they began when our people were trying to integrate. We tend to have a natural affinity for particular energies, magics you might say, whether that's through your family"—she gestured to me—"or through learning or experience... it's like any other craft really."

Ahead, I heard Drust grumble something about oversimplification, but Áine pointedly continued. "Anyway, these different forms tend to reflect their abilities or intentions. It's worth keeping in mind that their forms aren't actually shifting... now that you've felt your family's power, you're just seeing a different Aspect of them."

We trod along an even rockier track. In the dim light, I couldn't make out if there was a track or if the rocks and grasses had fallen conveniently in this layout. After a while, the balance tipped from whether it was worth turning back if I was unsure, to not knowing if I would even find my way back. The thickening trees, bushes, and rocks had homes at different heights around us. I followed the path Drust made ahead of me whilst Áine cast a shadow behind us, the guiding flames extinguishing as we passed. It made sense that the Seelie retreated to a place out of the world's way, but the same sense made me wonder whether it was all worth it anyway. What was their plan next to escape the situation they were in?

"Not far now," Áine called as it became more obvious that the cliff was running alongside us.

As I was about to acknowledge her, figures emerged from the darkness around us, the guiding flames lighting them only as they drew near. I shouted as the faceless figures came from the sides, above, and below us, their colourless clothing fading around them. Drust pushed me into Áine's arms. One had jumped from above us and landed where I had just been. I shook as Áine helped me catch my balance, my heart leaping with the strides my legs wanted to take. Six of them prowled around us in a circle. Spindly limbs dragged through the dirt. Jaws split open in their otherwise blank faces, broken up by needle-sharp teeth. Their features seared into my mind, as shouts and rough voices organised in sounds I didn't understand.

Áine pulled me along, undaunted. She dodged the one ahead of us, heading towards the mound at the end of the cleared pathway. Coordinated, Drust lunged for the same one, even as it lashed in our direction. Scuffles and the sounds of fighting tailed us. I had to trust Áine's hand briefly, needing to peer over my shoulder. The drumming inside my head and in my veins urged me to look, to watch.

Drust struggled behind us, locked in a skirmish with one of the figures, wielding two glinting knives I didn't even know he'd had. A figure lay in a heap behind us. Further back, the woods had come alive around the same women we'd seen before, as they stood in the trees. Their leaf-like hair rippled around them as brambles and weeds strung another one up, trapped. Three remained, snarling and swiping at the branches, until one of them pounced at the closest woman. I could feel my breaths suddenly, and the air caught in my throat as she fell. The maw closed around her beautiful features and I staggered, disbelieving. With a break from the onslaught, the other two twisted, refocusing.

I turned back, my shuffle becoming a sprint again, and saw the entrance to a tunnel rounding the edge of the cliff. As it became clearer, Drust shouted behind us. I didn't understand his words, but Áine pulled me forward before taking off her backpack and swinging it at one of the shadows chasing us. I stumbled and scrabbled. The grate nestled onto the cave's opening grew closer, whilst the echoing snarl of the remaining one behind me grew louder. I was sick at how useless I was in a truly threatening situation like this. My heartbeat thundered relentlessly in my ears.

The moment the figure reached me, a howl pierced through the night. I had to cover my ears, but the strength and pitch of it fractured through me. With some kind of recognition, the figure glanced between me and the cave entrance, and lunged for me the moment I'd paused. Long, sharp fingers gripped my coat. My breath was ragged with panic. I didn't have time to think. I turned sharply, trying to break the grip on me but hesitant to put any more of myself within its reach. When it began baring its teeth, some semblance of a smirk, the possibilities of what the Unseelie wanted with me came unbidden.

In desperation, I wrenched my coat away again, twisting its hand from me. My movements were frantic as I stumbled towards the grate. It grabbed my other hand. A chill, not unlike the one I felt around the darkness, slid down my neck. When I couldn't do anything else, I called out to the others and begged it to let me go. The key was heavy in my pocket, and I knew my father would've known what to do.

Chapter
Eight

In the moment between desperation and panic, I felt strangely delirious. The seconds stretched out, and the space between the beats of my heart lengthened. I knew our journey had been watched, I knew this was a determined attack before we were safely hidden away, and I knew that something had summoned the Unseelie. A dreamy haze fell over me, and the figures I saw lost their familiarity. I might have recognised them, but all I had to do, to name them, was wake up.

Guided by white flickering, three people trudged along a hidden path in the woods. A dark-haired male, a woman with bright hair the colour of dying leaves, and a woman with long hair and fringe swept to the side. The one who could wield the energy *it* needed. The van they had driven to this place was still.

Close to this place, there were waters it could use to travel back to him. The waters didn't hold enough energy for anything else; it couldn't harvest from them like it could from the other gates, like it could from her. It shifted back and spanned across farmland, back to the city it had first known, back to the dark-skinned figure that commanded their army. A woman stood to his right, her straight, dark hair limp against the sallowness of her skin. She continued addressing the commanders whilst the bald man paused, acknowledging its arrival and calling to the shadow that gathered around him.

Back where it had been directed to reap, support gathered at the edge of the trees. Lone figures came together and, carved into where their faces should've been, jaws stretched. Elongated features tasted the air. Long limbs navigated the rocks and gorse easily as they tracked the group that were so close to safety.

Chapter

Nine

Two slender white figures attacked from either side, shaking the darkness from me, overpowering it into submission. At first, I was thrown with my attacker, the daze dislodged from my mind and forgotten. My shoulder wrenched, and I stumbled once again. I thought they were both Oona until I caught my balance. One's ear was ragged, I noticed as I forced myself to move, and the other's head was narrower. Others from her pack?

By the time I reached the cave, Áine was close behind me again. I didn't pause to wonder if the grate would be locked. The guiding lights stopped nearby but, from the darkness, another light was being swiftly carried out from the cave. I quickly found Áine's look when the faint sound of boots met us at the entrance, not knowing whether this was anything to be worried about too. The metal was warm beneath my hand, and at her quick reassuring nod, it swung out easily when I pulled it.

Shapes in shining bronze and green leather uniforms moved from the darkness at a surprising pace, their weathered boots bore down on the compacted dirt. They adjusted as they jogged out to defend against those still fighting, though the featureless ones must have known they were outnumbered by then.

Áine leant to one side with me, out of the way, and we watched the lamplight spread. Drust emerged, he held a scrap of material to his head whilst he waded through the men and women who secured the area. He eyed Oona a step ahead of him, the shape of her jaw giving her away. Only then did I remember that her brothers and sisters had been here too, but when I looked around, I wasn't met with any other imperious stares.

"Wasn't there more of Oona's pack a moment ago?"

"She must have called for backup in case she wouldn't reach you in time. It was what alerted us too." I turned to see two women with the same face and dark skin coming towards us. The one who'd spoken had dark-brown hair wrapped around her head in a tight braid. The other's hair was a stark white in contrast and fell unadorned down her back, her eyes were also veiled in a white sheen but her gaze told me it would be foolish to think she was blind.

"Prime daughters, thank you for greeting us." Áine breathed deeply. "This is Peredur Woods' daughter. Morgan, this is Olwen and her twin sister, Lunete." She indicated to the women that a small number of the guards were surrounding, I realised suddenly that it was their brother who had sparked all this.

"Ms Woods, we regret that you've been involved in these attacks, but we hope our word of protection holds comfort, should you want it. We hope you might offer us your aid too. There's no need to decide now, of course. We can make a plan in the morning. We would like you to take comfort though— this does mean something." I heard Eoghan's words again as Olwen, the one with the braided hair, finished speaking. I should have been grateful, but my mind froze, needing time to process everything that had happened. If I couldn't help them, would they leave me in this mess by myself? Looking between them both, I watched the guards form another perimeter outside and felt for the two keys in my pocket, one for Rosie and one to return to my father's house. Drust came up behind Áine, the scuff he'd been tending on his head a moment ago reddened as the blood came to the surface.

Oona head-butted my hand, the snuffling wetness of her nose morphed into the crack of her skull. Surprised by her attention, I went to pet her more but stopped when her jowl rippled at me suddenly. She left my side as swiftly as she arrived. Was she still on guard? How had she arrived at this place so quickly?

"How did she know? How did she get here?" I asked.

"She has her own connection to the old magic," Lunete said from behind her sister's shoulder, her eyes still, the shadow of her pupils watched my direction. "Races like her are innately courtless, but there are those who use them for their own means. Her pack once belonged to one of our past kings. They were an Unseelie pack then but have since dispersed, only coming together when another of their kind needs them. There will only ever be one pack like them. Your family must have done something extraordinary to gain her loyalty."

I found Oona sitting not far from us, outside the guarded perimeter as she kept watch with them. Her red ears twitched and I felt a warm rush of gratitude and newfound respect. Had my father been the one that befriended her? Or a great grandparent? How long had my family protected their gate?

I inhaled suddenly, my eyes widening. "Doesn't that leave the gate unprotected?"

Olwen looked hesitantly to the guard closest to her. He cast his good eye over to Drust, who stood a pace away from us.

Drust looked over at the pause, his features shadowed outside the group's lamplight. "Freda Nic Díolmhain and Urien De Caimbeul will be able to hold it for a day, maybe two, but it would be safer to send help if there are those willing."

"I agree," Áine said. "Freda was able to reinforce some of the wards that were already there and Urien will know what to do if anything happens."

"Okay then, could you see who might be able to go? I believe the council would be unanimous in this," Olwen asked the same guard. She gestured to the passage they had come from. "Shall we? We can talk more about this at the morning assembly."

Light was sent forth into the blackness, away from the trees and leaf litter of the woods, away from the perimeter of guards and their discussions about protecting my father's ward. As we walked into the underpass, rocky avenues led away occasionally, but I no longer had the energy to ask if they joined back up again or led somewhere dangerously isolated. The leaping shadows slid over the formed rock, rough and natural. Mosses and tufts of sprouting grass lined the way, giving away the tunnel's age as it reminded me that they couldn't be the same shadows. Beyond the darkness, it smelt earthy and slightly stale, the chill in the air made it linger in my nose.

"Not that you'd know it was morning down here," I said, but the moment afterwards, I wondered whether it was insensitive, considering they didn't have anywhere else to go.

Ahead of me, Áine peered back and gave a grim smile. "It really isn't much further now." The tunnel widened out shortly after, stone formed a lip before opening up into a slightly larger cavern. It took a few more paces for me to realise that intermittent lanterns began on the other side, spaced out like the lampposts we had passed earlier. There was a visible patrol, where the light shone on smoothed rock and little else, but the tunnels continued past those in firm green leather.

"Oona?" I'd hoped she might stay, but when I turned to see what she was doing, she had already left. There was only the receding tunnel behind us. The dark closed in. The rock around me suddenly seemed closer, and the tunnel more ridged. I was unsure whether I felt more panic from the endless depth or at Oona's apparent prudence to leave the situation.

Drust shrugged as he caught up with me. "She won't go far. She must think you're in capable hands."

I looked back, the rest of the group waited near the lanterns that continued in.

"Come, you might be interested in this." Olwen called, gesturing me over.

Lunete hovered further in, hands on the rock wall and head inclined as if there was a whispering she couldn't quite make out. I stepped up to Olwen, expectantly, as though she were a tour guide, and I was ready to see the sights of any other culture. By the time we approached where Lunete listened,

I began to see outlined symbols marking the walls. Curving and dotted shapes bordered our way. Occasionally a detailed painting in faded, dusty beauty watched us go by.

"These were the original cave systems that our ancestors used to escape your land thousands of your years ago. We came from the north at first, hoping to find somewhere new. We lived in peace until the Unseelie King joined forces with a race of giants, and we were driven from where we'd settled again. This place was our home until the gatekeeper families, your family, found us somewhere new."

I felt an immediate tug from the wall we passed on our left. I slowed, looking at it more carefully as I walked. Lunete's eyes fell to me as her hand traced the same line of the rock face that pulled on my being.

"You can feel it, can't you?" Her voice was soft. "If you were to follow this vein of energy, it would lead you to the place that these families opened the first gates."

"And what d'you want me to do with it?" The question left me before I could even think about what that would imply, who said I'd be able to do anything with it?

Áine eyed the sisters and smiled. "We'll support you in what you want to learn and support you in what you don't want to do."

"It will be difficult for you, being so close to something that's been dormant for so long," Olwen added as the tunnel opened into an inconceivable chasm.

I probably gawked. My mind raced in the same way the stairways before me led in every direction. The entrance cavern was layered with stairs that led to arched doorways like a horizon of building fronts. I had to check the stalactites for their own stairs and hallways for one brief moment. The few flickering torches hinted at the late hour but also gave the cavern a sense of scale. Moons of flame hung on many of the stairways but not all. How could something like this exist outside the world I knew?

Drust came to a stop behind us, his voice closer and quieter than before. "Still also welcome to go on without us," he said, as always, offering the alternative perspective. I wondered if the others even heard him. It was a bizarre contrast against the Escher-style city rockscape ahead of us.

"H-how was this..." I couldn't begin to process the scale of what was hewn into the rock before us. "Was this all carved? How long were your people here?" Why would they live here for so long?

"It is said that many other races came to our aid, those skilled in working underground and architecture." Olwen looked between Áine and Drust when there was a natural pause. "Do either of you have the space to offer Ms Woods a few hours rest? It can be a point of discussion in the morning if needed."

Áine wrapped an arm around my shoulders. "My sisters and I will look after her."

I was in a dazed space between exhaustion and awe. The feel of her arm and chuckle felt distant, but I watched as they made arrangements for the morning. Olwen added when and where the meeting would be and some of the guards departed around us. Drust nodded at Áine, and his eyes settled on mine for half a moment before he turned. Walking around us, arm raised in a careful gesture, he edged past us towards the rock city. I felt the breath falter in my chest when he brushed by.

At that moment, his perceptive words and glances culminated into an enduring curiosity that settled inside me. I thought I saw the corner of Áine's mouth turn in a small grin.

"We'll see you in the morning, Ms Woods," Olwen said. Lunete threaded her arm with her sister's. "We don't have the luxuries we used to have, but we hope you'll be comfortable."

Awareness of my own silence grew alongside the unspoken words on my tongue. They were bitter, like the very feeling of expectation and condescending cordiality that lined my throat. I swallowed, feeling weary, and made a show of clearing it. "Thank you, just feeling that I'm safe is enough."

As I followed Áine, we passed simply carved rooms lit from within, and the sound of gentle, echoing snores. We passed awnings between pathways that created spaces for stalls and places to gather. We occasionally passed other people, those who inclined their head in greeting, as well as those who ducked further into their worn coats, silent. I noticed that nobody slept out in the open, bundled into sheltered corners, there were chambers for them and all the belongings they'd carried this far.

"There's enough space for everybody," Áine said. "It's kind of interesting the way everyone's chosen their new homes to be honest. Some races have found support together, some families have split and found the most remote spaces, others have decided it's time to become courtless. This isn't the only camp either. Other members of the council oversee other temporary homes. I don't think they'll all be at the meeting tomorrow, but they try to meet every month or so."

I didn't know whether that would work in my favour or not. I shifted the small backpack around on my shoulder. The weight was a comfort. There were fewer stairways the further we walked, but we passed just as many doorways until the faint sound of water greeted us from around a corner. A water pump sat at the centre of the space, contrasting with the worn, ancient etchings on the walls around us. A man filled his roughly carved jug whilst a handful of Aspects queued patiently behind him. Cloaked women with protruding, fin-like ears, and a long-haired, bearded man with curving horns wrapped around his head waited behind them. The flowing heartbeat of the pump added normality and comfort to the silence.

"It's channelled from an underground river. If you keep going west, you'll head right into the waterfall. Would you like to freshen up?" She said suddenly, half turned into a set of stairs. "We're just up here."

I wondered what modern conveniences I'd unthinkingly left behind but nodded. I channelled the camping experiences I'd had without Rosie. "That'd be great."

She changed direction and started down the stairs instead. I wasn't yet comfortable being in the earth without using my hand to guide myself along the rock, even as my spare hand found my pocket and clutched my keys. I had to remind myself that I hadn't agreed to anything yet.

Buntings of light accented the varied strata, layers of brown and grey felt homely in the way a cocoon might. There were plain symbols painted on the entrances and corners of the levels back up— leaves, trees or animals, in ochres, greens and yellows. I could only assume they might be street names or guidance of some kind.

By the time we made it to entrances with fabrics drawn over them, like tents over the archways, I was beginning to desperately hope for sleep. I couldn't imagine that the sun had risen, but it still felt early when it gradually got busier. Time jumped in fractions, moments where I had switched off, until Áine paused outside one such doorway. She smiled in a friendly way and indicated quiet, reminding me of the sisters she'd mentioned.

"If it's okay with you, you can use my bed tonight, I think there's an extra blanket, and I'll sneak in with one of the girls. We can go about finding you one tomorrow."

It was dark inside and a vague scent of soap clung to the shadowed outlines of a layout. Before Áine replaced the curtain behind us, the little light that stole through allowed me to glimpse the open space. Towards the back of the cave, two heavily breathing shapes were laid on raised platforms. Áine rummaged gently in a trunk that sat between the two platforms, then carried something over to the empty one for me. I dropped my bag near my feet when she laid what looked like a blanket onto the bed.

"I'll just be over there, let me know if you need anything," she whispered, her face all in shadow.

I waited until I could no longer make out what she was doing, and then I sat down and began undoing my shoes. Bringing my bag beside me, I felt around for the bottle I'd refilled and quietly took a drink whilst backing up against the rock face. Though we'd been walking around for a while now, I thought I'd begin to feel the chill in the earth, against the rock, but I couldn't. On the contrary, there was a close heaviness in the air that lulled me further to sleep. I felt my face relax and didn't realise that I'd been guarding my expression. My eyes heated and itched suddenly. I took a deep breath, drew my knees up onto the platform with me and must have fallen straight to sleep.

Chapter
Ten

The moment I was conscious again, I wondered how long I could get away with keeping my eyes closed. I heard murmuring but couldn't make out the sounds enough to discern any words. My brain was still dusty with sand and, at first, I only remembered the car journey before registering higher, younger voices.

Something clutched my insides when the thought of waking up coalesced. I stayed where I was, an ear tuned into how urgent Áine and her sisters' voices were. Áine spoke quietly and sensibly, the voice of someone who'd taken on the caring role. I was intruding. Did they know why Áine went away? Where were their parents? The only trace I could draw on was the evacuations, I knew some people hadn't escaped. It reminded me of the Unseelie I'd already encountered, what would be left of Falias city if they returned? How would they continue their lives?

I needed to stretch. From the position I had slept in, keys dug into my thigh, and I could feel the weight of my phone resting on me. I hadn't turned it off, a stupid mistake that would cost me battery life. I hadn't seen anything electrical on the way in. I took a deep breath and stretched my legs, giving my new roommates a chance to notice before I stepped on any other unspoken courtesies.

For the normally dreary time between winter and spring, it was still surprisingly cosy. One of the lanterns that lit our way was dimmed, and light danced on the soft blanket coverings on the other side and a makeshift table that was propped up between two chests. On the other side of the table, one of the girls sat among a layout of cushions with a chunk of charcoal, and she drew on the wall that separated the beds. She only looked about six or seven. Áine knelt at the table with her other sister, a slightly older girl about thirteen or fourteen, they were slicing portions of dark wholemeal bread. Two quartered apples and a jug that looked like the one the man had used at the water pump sat beside them already.

"Good morning," the younger girl said in my direction, her accent rested heavily on the 'r' but she was still perfectly understandable. The others chimed in as soon as they realised who she was talking to.

"How did you sleep?" Áine poured some water into one of the nearby bowls and offered it from where she was before placing it closer to me on the table.

I nodded and smiled in what I hoped was a sleepy, positive manner rather than a grimace. As politely as possible, I slipped the top half of my phone out and turned it off. The lack of bars at the top of the screen told me it wouldn't be of any use down here anyway. "I was so tired, I think I would have slept through anything."

"That's probably the best way to do it." She smiled back. "Ruari, Emer, this is Morgan, we'll be sharing what we have with her for a little while. Don't mind them if they ask some strange questions, this is their first trip to your country."

After a small breakfast, Áine showed me more of the cave city, Pelthas. We had time to spare before the meeting, though I hadn't yet worked out how she knew that.

"So, if I followed the symbol with three trees, it would lead me back outside?" I asked.

"They lead you to where we've revived the ancient farms. I heard they were pretty inaccessible if you haven't already gone through Pelthas though. I'm sure we'll be able to take a look at some point if you want. There's some grassland there too that's a popular spot in the evening."

After eating and freshening up, her sisters went to a gathering at the district hub to see if they were needed for the day. Along the way, they had explained it was how the work was divided. Emer, the youngest, had been looking forward to their afternoon classes.

It was busier around this time. Shards of light fell from the hollow precipice above and made it bright enough to see the races that passed on different levels of the other side of the cavern. Many carried their lamps, as well as baskets and boxes filled with the day's work. We walked by many others chatting or setting up basic stalls, who barely gave us a second glance as we walked. We passed close enough to see what people were doing and catch the lilting language that was occasionally familiar to me. Blunt, short noises and meaningful hand signs punctuated the air. They were trying to settle into something like normality.

"Do they produce enough to feed everyone? The farms?" We headed further towards the centre. If I looked across the space in the direction we'd entered, I thought I could make out the tunnel that led back to the woods.

"Not entirely yet. It must have done before though. We supplement it with what we can get outside or from nearby towns. We've been helped by people already living here too, where they can." For a moment, I thought she meant those living in the caves, but there must have been other courtless living nearby. "But I don't know an awful lot about how that's all done."

"You think it's the same with the other camps?"

She grew pensive, and I began to think I might need to say something placating, my own scold as hot as anybody else's. But then she shrugged. "I hope so. If that's all we have after not knowing what we were going to go, it's something we can build on. Everyone just wants time to work things out, enjoy what they have. Some people"—she gave me a look from the side of her eye—"like Drust... are still sending messages out to find their family."

For the first time that day, I noticed the walking aids and bandages hidden underneath the unfamiliar styles of clothing, the determination to keep going.

"I'm sorry you all had to go through something like this. There's so many people..." Unexpectedly, I wanted to be able to do something for them, and even though he hadn't shown any sign of needing it, for Drust. I asked quietly, "Do they know about numbers?"

"Nothing confirmed, it's probably hard to be accurate when you don't know how many citizens couldn't leave."

The coldness of the shadow and laughter of the gang in the park passed by me, and I wondered how much folklore was actually true. What else did the Unseelie keep around them? And if I hadn't gotten myself muddled in all this, would I have cared in the same way?

"Please tell me if this is an awful thing to ask... I get the impression attacks like this are cyclical, but what made this time so much worse? How did they take Falias this time?"

She looked around the largest open space we had walked through yet and then back at me. At the base of the far side, water flowed over a raised platform of rock, creating a flush of greenery and a queue that waited for water. Around the space, other groups congregated with polite distances between them. The stream led around a portion of the cavern wall, before leading away. In the middle, guarded by a fairy-circle of smaller rocks, a blackened stain was being swept out. The whole space could easily hold all the people I'd seen so far.

Áine pulled me out of the main path that others walked, and we stopped away from anyone else. A handful of steps away was the only other carved entrance I could see, and the arch opened up into another vast space where people were beginning to meet.

"Council members, masters, people of high renown don't often change their political interests, but the noble son did for some reason, and who better for"—she lowered her voice again—"the Unseelie to rally behind. Who knows what that means for us? As well as brute force, they have the law; he is the firstborn. They rose up, the Unseelie, about twenty years ago in our country. Some people think the council could've done a bit more but ultimately the Seelie's interests are still the same, which is why most people are here."

I was reminded of Eoghan's advice and matched Áine's tone. "What more could the council do?"

She waved to someone that headed past and into the proceeding cavern but continued, "Lunete's an oracle. It's known that when she was a girl, she foresaw her brother's shifting to the Unseelie. Apparently, that's part of the reason why Eoghan chose to leave and become courtless— something to do with her prophecy. But the point is, they had the information, but struggled to know whether they should change the way he was raised or not."

The role that Eoghan had in all this struck me, the casual welcome he'd given me when there were only certain people that would've sought my father's house out. Whose perspective held fewer lies? Then the rest of what Áine had said followed, and I couldn't hold my disbelief back at the idea of prophecies. I looked around again, taking in the obviously worn homespun clothes and the occasional long, wide-sleeved outfit, and shrugged it away to process later.

"Shall we?" she said, indicating to the adjacent cavern. "You've probably realised it won't be in English, but I'll try to translate the important bits."

• • • •

"Greetings to everyone," Áine whispered to me, translating the rhythmic words. "Today we have Belenus, Master of Accords, Enid, Master of Balance, Agrona, Master of Alliance, and Lunete, Master of Vision, here to discuss the Unseelie and what our next step might be..."

As I listened, I explored those sat around us. We had walked around and through islands of rock benches that led to an open space in the middle of it all. Many of the benches were still connected, but there were also many people who remained standing or sat cross-legged in smooth, eroded spaces. Those who sat closer to the inner circle, where the council sat, had fewer patches in their clothes and the material appeared finer from where I was. But as individuals spoke and added their questions to the discussion, it seemed that everyone had an equal chance of speaking. Áine couldn't translate everything, though.

I registered a familiar shape and set of features in my peripheries, his dark hair framing the face that looked a different way. Even when part of me remained aware of what my subtle movements were doing, I turned my focus back to the council that would decide if I were to stay.

"...this man is giving his account of something that happened to him on the way here... Agrona is asking someone to take notes of it to investigate, defence falls under her responsibility too," Áine continued. After she'd had time to listen to what was happening next, she said, "Oh, that's us."

My heart thudded and I tensed at the idea of having to speak to everyone. "What?!"

Her wide eyes mirrored my own. "It's fine, don't worry, we can go up and just speak to the council if you'd rather." The relief pressed into my lungs.

"Come on," said a voice I hadn't heard that day. Drust stepped up to us. "I don't need to give them another reason to not listen to me."

"Why wouldn't they—" I began when Áine raised her hand and started forward. We hadn't been positioned far from the front but the extra few rows that passed felt like the rest of the cave system. I kept my eyes on the five council members that sat in a semi-circle ahead, their attention on us equally. They looked to Áine. She in turn cleared her throat and initiated the discussion in something I could understand.

"The Woods' Gate has also been a target for the shadow. Peredur was clever enough not to leave it unprotected, however the Gwyn's hound that provided some protection has thought it best to keep an eye on his daughter, Morgan Woods, instead. We thought it prudent to consult for further opinions but initially believed it would be safer for all to allow Miss Woods to accompany us. The rest of our team, Freda Nic Díolmhain and Urien De Caimbeul, remained with the gate and have support on the way."

"Would you remind us why you believed the shadow was also after Miss Woods?" Agrona directed a hard stare over to where Drust stood, even though I knew we'd spoken about it before. It provoked a different reaction in him, different to how he'd acted back at the house and to when Olwen and Lunete had greeted us. He stared back at Agrona, his hands held behind his back, stood formally with one knee slightly bent. I wondered why he'd be as nervous as I was though.

"We were able to help Miss Woods when she was attacked away from the house. Until recently, we assumed it had been the first time, however she reports that there was another time." He watched their responses, most of them nodding as if this was acceptable, he continued. "We also thought this was curious, considering her link to the old magic."

An unnaturally slender woman from one of the front rows raised her arm to speak. "That's your area of expertise, is it not, Drust Nidhir? Was this your idea?" Others along the same row gave her a look that told me there was more context here.

Drust appeared unfazed. "It was but upon sharing it with my team and those whose opinions we'd sought, it was also the most plausible explanation."

"And something worth looking into more," the council woman Enid said. "Nidhir, have you any thoughts about what the Unseelie might be able to do with this source of energy?"

I saw his eyes flick to Áine and over to Belenus, the council member who had been at the original meeting, "There has been an idea that takes the time rift into account. The only thing that has been able to do something like this and used the same energy is the Stone of Fál—" A quiet echo in the front rows sounded, a reminder that the rest of the crowd was listening in.

"Council," Agrona interrupted, "it ought to be noted that this idea came from exile Eoghan Wilkins, as well as a Nidhir presenting this idea." As the whispering echo grew, I was certain she'd spoken louder than was necessary.

Belenus then spoke just as clearly. "It must also be noted that, considering a prophecy reevaluation is imminent, Wilkin's position may still be as honest as you or I. And even if Nidhir is a very patient and convincing Unseelie informer, we at least have some sort of starting point." Belenus looked at the council member next to him, and I thought I could make out his eyes roll.

Olwen cleared her throat suddenly and, over the resounding mutters around us, said, "Please continue."

Drust's face had hardened, and I wondered if Áine would tell me the things he was setting his jaw against saying. He inclined his head briefly at Olwen and Lunete before resuming. "It was suggested that the prime son may have created this shadow with his past actions, as it would allow him to gather the power needed to wake the stone. His actions may have started a ripple, and who knows what that darkness could do to the gates?" I looked at him just as he paused, his expression shifted. "A breakdown of the connection."

A man from the crowd stood, looking both ways around the pensive faces, "Isn't it obvious? It sounds like the solution to this theory is to find a way to impede the shadow, and so far, I can't see that being a bad next step in any situation."

All these details sounded urgent and much too large for any one of us to deal with on our own. With every response, the more I felt that I hadn't received safety at all. Both situations, with or without the council, filled me with such heavy dread, I didn't know which I preferred. In a moment of silence, I felt compelled to ask something that nobody had covered yet.

"Am I allowed to know what this stone actually does?" I looked at each of the council as they turned to face me. "I mean, I'm aware that it gave you your world, Albios, but what other possibilities are we talking about here?" I suddenly felt recklessly confident in what I deserved to know, and how I acted wouldn't change what I could and couldn't do. Áine was obviously biting back a grin, and it told me I would be fine.

Lunete was the first one to reply to me, her voice more accented than other members, like Áine's sisters. "The energy you might see as magic feeds on the natural inclination of the user. Are you more likely to help up a blind lady or leave her? Would you give happiness to yourself or to others? We hold nothing against those who choose the middle ground, those who are courtless. They may come and go as they please because fundamentally, it's the connection we share that binds us. With this, we can influence potentials, luck, health, and as I'm sure you can imagine, this ends up being a scale.

"Artefacts like the stone have gone through so many generations, we can't be sure anymore where they come from. But when they access enough power, they can manipulate the larger forces: life, time."

"Well, what have they tried to do before? I've been told they had a setback not long ago?"

Their eyes queried each other before Enid sat up, "Not as in the dark as we've been led to believe, are you?"

I didn't want my sudden curiosity to count against me, but I also wasn't sure how much the others had been allowed to tell me. "My father kept records... what I could read of them."

"A few intolerant families thought they deserved more than the rest of us," Belenus said. More than a couple of faces around us darkened and found something interesting in their notes. As if trying to steer topics, he then added, "But I agree that stopping the shadow should be our first priority. We might have more time to find out why in the meanwhile."

"What would you like from us, Miss Woods?" As soon as Olwen said it, I knew it was the moment that Eoghan had warned me about.

"I don't know," I admitted. I couldn't tell whether the murmurs around us were from boredom or the subject matter. Would this affect many of them? How many of them would I actually meet?

"Nidhir," Enid said, "would you be in a suitable position to direct Miss Woods in her discovery of the old magic?"

For a moment, Drust hesitated. The pause felt like a hint that he'd rather be focusing on other work, but he still responded, "Of course." He lowered his gaze from the council politely, though didn't look my way.

"Ó Cuileáin, Miss Woods has a place with you, I believe?" Olwen said, and when Áine confirmed, she continued. "It might be a good idea if she's able to join your sparring time too? If you have time, Miss Woods, it might be easier for the time being and will help you defend yourself."

Lunete's lilting tones drifted around us again and what tension remained, dispersed. "I would also appreciate some time with you, how much we could both learn." A little doubt gnawed at the back of my mind. What did I have to teach? But what else would I be doing here? And they knew it.

The council in the carved seats ahead began exchanging looks as if they were about to move on. Was that it?

"What about Mr. Wilkins?" I said louder than I intended, and the surprise at myself was warm in my cheeks.

Olwen cast a question to the man at her side. "Eoghan Wilkins?"

"Prime daughter," Belenus responded at a respectful volume, turning to face Olwen, "Wilkins was implicated in one of Lunete's foretellings. The decision was made between himself and your father. He did so willingly, but it's probable that Wilkins would have remained on the council."

"We would hear everyone's thoughts. Belenus, Agrona, I fear I only remember a few details from this, would you remind us later?"

Chapter
Eleven

S hortly after Áine had shown me where many people set up
their stalls for trading, a bell echoed throughout the
tunnels. Many people moved, which made me think it was a
warning, attacks outside couldn't be uncommon. When others
didn't look up from their wares, still sat on carved rock or leant
against the walls, I finished looking at a basket of braided
crowns that were being traded for their upcoming spring
celebration. I caught up with Áine who browsed a little further
in.

"Should I be worried about that bell?"

"What?" she said, looking around for the threat. "Oh, the
bell? It's for lunch— you hungry?"

After stopping off at 'home' for our eating utensils, we
made our way back to the large open space outside the council
chamber. The crush of people told me why some had waited
with their stalls. On the opposite side to where the queue for
water was, long, low tables were laid out with basic foods.
Chunks of dense-looking bread sat alongside piles of apples,
and further down, cauldrons of stew were ladled into waiting
bowls. I didn't miss the occasional guard who stood behind
those helping.

There were no other tables set out, so after getting their food, people dispersed back into the tunnels or out the way the farms and grassland were. The space didn't seem to get any emptier whilst we waited, though. After claiming our share, we decided to head outside and find a spot in the nearby field.

"We all eventually have our turn with food, even the council," Áine said as we walked. "It's a bit of a chore, so it usually means you get to eat first and finish the day early."

"Sounds like a bit of a chore to organise this many people too." I chewed a bite of the bread. It had such a dark, earthy flavour, I had to clear my throat. I put it in my stew with hopes of making it more palatable.

She smiled and nodded. "It's divided into districts and then the hubs do the rest. It's not a job I'd enjoy, but some people love that stuff."

The exit opened up at the lowest point of the rolling hills, the white-cloaked sky obscuring any sun trying to break through. I wrapped my hands around the wooden bowl, warming them against the typically-March day. The view flattened out in between, and spanning down the valley as far as I could see, cultivated land lay in every state between being turned over and neatly growing leafy greens. People tended the ground in most of these too. Without the sun, the mountains around us didn't look high enough to veil it all, but, at the same time, I couldn't hear any roads. Only birdsong. At the edges of the managed land, bunches of daffodils gave me the sun that I'd been hoping for.

As we made our way to the grassy expanse opposite, Áine said, "It's warded, of course, as you might imagine. Not too dissimilar to the ones your father used, except if anyone comes across it, they come out the other side. I think it's been officially mapped like that and everything."

We found a space to sit and, although it was damp and a little muddy, nobody seemed to mind. I scooped my coat underneath myself as I sat.

"You think I could go walking then? How much of it is protected?" I sipped from my bowl and saw other people using their bread as a spoon for the chunks. Further down, I could just make out people sparring, and Áine pointed past them.

"I think it's a little further than them, but probably best to stay on this side to be safe."

Pulling my legs closer to shield against the cold, I quietly asked, "Áine? How long was the last war?" How long could I be here?

She looked back, and I could see in her forehead that she was trying to work out a response. "It was a little bit different without the shadow, but there were reports of Unseelie attacks for about three years after. For us, it's only about six-hundred years since our land, Albios, was founded and as far as I know... Pelthas here hasn't been needed since. I guess the small blessing from the time rift is that it won't be an extraordinary amount of time for your life here..."

We finished off our stew, I resorted to using my fingers. As we ate, the world around me faded into the distance. I stared at the food, and the flavours and textures registered as little as the background noise. I hadn't had concrete plans, but the ability to make them and choose disappeared as I registered what she'd said. It could have been twenty years away from their families if the time rift was active.

"Occasionally the cities do change courts, but the last Seelie-Unseelie Pact lasted the longest so far. Essentially, whilst the Seelie were in court, the Unseelie had their choice of positions. That might sound detrimental, it's worth remembering that it was still under a Seelie Council though. There was a man called Llyr, a direct descendant of one of the old families, and he started feeding them this idea that the Unseelie were entitled to more. They wanted to change the system and suddenly didn't like being reliant on the Seelie, until one night they nearly killed the council in their sleep.

"Lunete was still young, but the hints she gave saved them. She's been a huge influence on the Seelie since then and eventually took up the Master of Vision post. But I think Olwen's more suited as Prime Figure, really."

"The Unseelie must really want Lunete out the way then," I said under my breath as we got up. She gave me a grim smile before we started back, there were still afternoon duties before we could rest. The field was beginning to clear.

"As far as I know, all the people involved were executed. Geraint, the Prime Father before, wanted to set an example with them." She lowered her voice. "Drust's blood family... his grandfather was the one who let them into the prime house."

I gave her a return look that was supposed to mean 'you can't just drop that in there', but she shook her head and guided us to a place to wash our bowls. The more I heard as we descended into the tunnels again, the more I felt that old familiar weight settle on my shoulders.

••••

After dropping off our bowls, we continued to the district hub further down the passage that held our room. It ended up being larger than some of the individual chambers I'd seen and, as we entered, Emer waved from the group of children she was sat with. We approached the back of the cavern where lamps hanging on hooks lit up a circle of adults sat on the opposite side. Most of them sat on a woven mat with two of the older ones on basic stalls. They all worked between supermarket notebooks, quietly conferring. They all greeted us when Áine approached. A bearded man smiled.

"Iùrnan, Barra, Mairéad, Ailish, Guaire, how do you find yourselves?"

"Áine!" One of the women said and then spoke in the same rhythmic language I'd heard up until this point. Áine answered in the same, and they had a short chat before she gestured to me. "This is Morgan, she'll be staying with us for the time being. I'm just showing her around today, but she'll be an extra pair of hands. She'll need to fit in sparring and two other meetings every couple of days though. Can we give her tomorrow to settle in, and then start to schedule her afterwards?"

The other woman nodded and rapidly summarised to the others. "Welcome. Come with the girls, and by then, we'll have something." Then, turning back to Áine, she said, "You have time? Taraghlan is down hands on blankets?"

"No problem." She looked at me. "It'll give you an introduction of sorts."

As I followed, I watched as she checked in with two families along the way. They had all been bound together by close living quarters, and the assistance they offered each other was traded just like the wares below. We turned the corner to see another group, all at different stages of working wool—pulling it apart, spinning it. Before Áine engaged in conversation with a man, presumably Taraghlan, she showed me how to tease the coarse wool out.

Like old friends, their heads bent together in earnest discussion. Every now and then though, Áine checked in and recapped very briefly. I began to notice commonplace words. The weaver, an elderly man with silver hair and nimble fingers, explained how his daughter had decided to be courtless. He looked weary.

It was mindless work, and soon a palpable heaviness began to settle on my own spirit. It whispered that I wasn't doing enough, that I would be a burden to these people.

Eventually, Áine turned the conversation to their upcoming Ēostre celebration, which I took to be their spring celebration, and alternated between English and their national language, Sindaric, again. They were looking forward to decorating with spring flowers, and lighting carved candles at the big bonfire dance.

Chapter
Twelve

Áine guided me to the next day's meeting place. While we waited for Drust, she told me that the nearby grassland was being used as an informal exercise and training space during the day. To our right, a group in rough-spun trousers sparred, their torsos bare and bruised from the edges of their hands. Up ahead, distant enough that their features blurred, pairs drifted through synchronous shapes together, the speed of the transitions varied to a beat only they could hear.

Drust finally arrived, and apprehension flitted in my stomach. He started talking as soon as Áine headed back, a heavy frown on his face. "The first thing about what you would call magic is that it's not adding luck, health, or advantage to the world. Like any other force, we can only act as conduits to redirect it. Many would say our highest priority is being a good judge of who is deserv—"

I attempted to see how dark his rainclouds were by raising my hand, he looked over and there was no give in his eyes. I could tell that he would rather be doing something else.

"What're you doing?"

"If you need to do other things, I don't want to stop you from doing them," I said.

"It's not that simple." He looked above me for a second and swallowed. "I'd be in the same situation if I helped you or not, waiting on news from other camps, trying to find out more about the time rift... We're all trying to find our families."

The heaviness sat in my stomach this time, and blood thudded into my face. "I know, I'm sorry. I only meant, if you really don't want to do this, I'm sure I'll manage somehow if the situation calls for it."

"Then I would think you're also underestimating the situation."

In reality I knew I'd stay and do what I had to, even if it meant that their wards were still protecting me. He let out a deep sigh.

"So do you think you could do anything right now?" Drust said. We already stood a small distance away from anyone else.

I tried to keep the scepticism out of my voice. "Honestly, probably not. It all happened so quickly, and this has all been so disorientating. I—"

"I'm not here to spy on you either. You don't need to think of excuses for me. This would be much more natural for both of us if you're honest with me." I felt my resolve harden, I suddenly didn't care if I could or I couldn't do anything. Whatever energy I could syphon into didn't change the danger that everyone was in, the danger people he loved were in.

"And what if that still doesn't help?"

He raised an eyebrow at me. "Then we would've wasted less time by going round in circles."

The open space we stood in wasn't far from the edge of the farmland Áine had shown me a couple of days ago. The edge of the protective ward wasn't far past them, but I could still make out the familiar green uniform in the distance. I wasn't sure how to feel about being guarded. We had been safe, as my hosts had promised, but I was just in another system. Only in this one, I knew hardly any of the rules.

Ruari and Emer had shown me where to get daily rations from and where to trade for any little luxuries. Where one person found value in particularly smooth branches, another was appreciative of the extra bread. They also showed me where they went most days to be given a task to help with. Ruari couldn't explain it fully, but she got me to understand that there was a structure. They showed me where everybody could gather in the evenings, if they wanted, to find support, to sing and dance, to laugh. I couldn't help but wonder what their city had been like.

"I remember feeling like my life was over," I said finally. "It attacked me, and it was like the gate protected me, not the other way around." There was more admittance in those words than I'd intended. His brown eyes bore straight back at me when he shrugged.

"Well, that's just basic theory. These things remain inactive when untouched. It couldn't have done something without you either."

Drust and I hadn't purposefully seen each other since I'd been here. Most of my time had been spent with Áine or her sisters. I'd found few precious moments when I could explore by myself, but that seemed to get the odd curious look from Áine. People checking in. But I could spend a little more time around him, if he wanted to.

"This isn't going to be one of those situations where you scare me into a reaction, is it?"

He gave a small smirk. "I'd thought about it."

I thought back to the moment everything had gone black and felt a little sick. The utter absence of anything that made me seek the power that eventually replied, in exchange for the conscious eternity of not knowing if I could come back. I wasn't sure, and had yet to find the moment to ask, whether the group of gatekeepers that I was part of could even influence anything if they weren't near gates. Drust's undertone said I should be able to find the path back, that I should always be able to save myself.

"I don't know where to even begin." I realised I expected another smirk, but his utter focus took me by surprise.

"It's like listening, there's a thrum under the silence and it wants to be heard. Only you're listening beyond your senses, it's not actually beating aloud and you're the one it can whisper through. Does that make any sense?"

"I'm not sure." A breath of amusement escaped me and, whilst I worked through what he meant, I felt my attention separate. I was reminded of the pull I'd felt from the tunnels. I found my left hand in my coat pocket. Usually buttoned safe, I rubbed my finger over Rosie's key. I didn't have anything to lose in trying. Resting further in the hollow of my pocket, the heavy brass key I'd found on the dashboard grazed the back of my hand, leaving a cold path. I pulled my hand back in surprise, thinking about the thrum he'd spoken of.

In a quiet voice, I asked, "Do you ever get the urge to whisper like an Unseelie?"

"Why?" His voice was loud and hard in contrast. For a fraction of time, I couldn't tell if it was in laughter or anger. My heart jumped in my throat when I realised. "What has Áine been telling you now?"

"Nothing." My blood drummed with a need to clarify under the disbelief in his expression. "What do you mean? What has she been telling me already?"

His jaw tightened, as if displaying more of himself had been unintended. Nobody around us had been close enough to notice the outburst, but I immediately connected his sudden inflection with Agrona's previous attitude and what Áine had told me. I had meant it in regards to myself, even if I was curious about what he might say.

"Why would you ask that?" Though his voice was lower, its intensity had concentrated.

"Well, I could put some of it together from the council meeting. I don't think she really likes me that much either."

His face softened slightly when he understood I was speaking in a personal manner. "People will think what they will. The hard part is having confidence in what you believe yourself to be, regardless of what they might think."

I kept quiet, not knowing how to respond.

"We can't get much stronger if we face what we fear about ourselves, even when there's some awful stuff out there too." A recovering grin hitched his lips on one side. The moment passed, and I knew I should have asked another question but still didn't know what. I didn't know what to think anymore. Like the rising walls of the valley we were in, the enormity of the situation that I'd been drawn into closed around me.

"Hey, if you find any other objects of interest, you let me know. I'd love to be the one to show Agrona that acorn hoard."

"I don't know how likely that is," I said, unsure when I would, in fact, return to my father's house. "And why wouldn't I keep all that glory for myself?"

"You've already offered them something quite important. If that hasn't helped, I don't know what will."

I smiled back and gave him a friendly shove as he smirked at my reaction.

• • • •

Over the following couple of weeks, I discovered the flare in Drust's eyes when he wanted me to try something different. Some days he arrived withdrawn— those days he normally left early, but other days, he was earnestly focused on helping. He often worked through his ideas once we'd established where we were, dividing his attention between me and far in the distance.

At first, he made sure I understood the basics of how we were able to manipulate these forces. We then tried channelling through strong emotion, like when I was fearing for my life, and what he called energy transference, where he attempted to guide it through me instead. I tried to remain open, but had difficulty concentrating when his firm, warm touch held either side of my face. I don't think he was particularly swayed. He also talked about visiting Pelthas' site of old magic. It was a place of respect and visitations were recorded, so we had to wait and hear back from the council. Áine laughed when I spoke about it all in the evenings. From what I gathered afterwards, much of his work in Falias was researching what they could do and how their sacred artefacts worked.

I started my days early. Ruari and Emer were always quiet but, as if a piece of me was tuned into any disturbance, I was awake as soon as they started moving. They didn't leave without me, and I was expected to help with spring celebration preparations as part of their household. On our way, we'd often see other families carrying food, supplies, or helping out with cleaning and decorating. There were just as many tending crops or tending the disabled and elderly, like we did. By late morning, I was usually eager to get out into the valley, not just to spend some time to myself, but to familiarise myself with the caverns and tunnels and see what I could find. Even on Drust's absent days, I would stay out in the valley, people watching as they sparred, playing, or sat contemplating on their own too. The suffocating press felt more manageable outside, the jar lifted for a short time.

After lunch, and an hour or so to myself, Áine would always find me. She wanted to hear about everything, in her bubbly, interested way of drawing information from people. Occasionally she talked about something that happened in the cave systems, families that had been reunited or ones that decided the courts were no longer for them, or recent attacks that increasingly happened outside; and some of the names were no longer strangers to me.

Chapter
Thirteen

By the time Ēostre arrived, spring was truly making an appearance. Bright sunshine made its way through the rocky fractures and Fibonacci fern ringlets began to unfurl outside. Lanterns lit up the art people had painted from clays and berry dyes along the walls and above archways. Entwined line designs wrapped around small flowers and hares stretched in the general direction that everyone was going. Laughter carried through the open hallways and added something to those who wore their best clothes. They greeted each other as if they'd lived there all their lives, children darted between those who stood waiting for others, as well as those who headed in the direction of the open cavern outside the council space.

Áine, Ruari, and Emer had gone early, in their prettiest dresses. Emer wanted to help finish the decorations, and who was I to pass up some space? Áine gave me a don't-worry-I-understand grin and said she'd meet me by the farm passage when food was ready. I didn't know how I would know when the food was ready but decided to keep watch for eager buffet faces.

I had very quickly gone through the clothes I'd managed to fit in my backpack. I'd borrowed a couple more and tried to keep an eye out for what people traded, but that day, I made sure I was in a fresh shirt. Combing my fingers through my hair, I took in the music that a trio played on hand-drums just where the tunnel opened up. It looked like people had milled around enough that there was space, and nearer the way in from the woods, a white flash caught my eye. Stepping out from the drip of people, I followed the direction she'd gone.

I'd only seen Oona a couple of times since arriving. It felt like she'd kept her distance for a reason, but no one was sure whether it was the crowded nature of the caves, the fact that they were closed off, or something else entirely. I didn't blame her. I couldn't help but eye the way she had entered myself. Not for the first time, I thought about what I was doing here. If I knew how, I would help these people, rather than just drain their resources. I could look after myself. Except if I did, oblivion waited. And where was the edge of their generosity? Like I found myself doing more and more, I brushed the edge of my father's key with the hope that I would find some of his courage.

Oona sat overlooking the stairways and passages, like she had when we first arrived. I approached her, walking against those heading further in but stopped a few strides out. I could make out her narrow face. She was focused on me like I was her— a ripple in her jowl sent a momentary shiver down my spine. Her gentle imperiousness returned when I stopped drawing closer. I didn't understand and a tightness gripped under my throat. Had I broken whatever loyalty she had to my father? I looked around briefly and felt that everything was still safe, so tried again, hoping it had been a misunderstanding.

It wasn't. She snarled again, and I wondered if she was trying to prevent me from leaving. I knew I wasn't going to leave in that moment, but I also couldn't face impacting Oona's acceptance of me. I stood still, uselessly trying to transmit to her that I only wanted to go to her, until I was accidentally jostled by the crowd. She left my sight for a second and was gone after the figure had apologised to me.

After I lost sight of her, I meandered back to the open cavern with the water running through it. Groups of people grew louder, laughter flowed as free as the water, and the odd shout rose to be heard. I watched as the people around me remembered some of their own substance. Suddenly, I couldn't imagine *not* exploring who I was further, as if collecting different experiences would help me find me that little bit quicker.

The smaller circle of rocks at the centre of the cavern guarded a fire on this occasion. It warmed up the space, even as the chasm above drew the smoke out. It was crowded but still seemed less lively than I'd expected, and nobody looked particularly hungry yet, so I took the time to continue walking around. Before the rock face covered with water, a row of barrels lined the edge near the entrance. Rough mugs, often used at meal times, had been laid out on a nearby table for everyone to use. I watched someone else go first before letting my hand reach for one.

Enid was the first one to break my solitude and make her way over. She greeted me in Sindaric, one of the phrases I'd picked up, and continued in something I fully understood. "I hope you have fun at our humble gathering. It happens to be my favourite from across the year, we're always planning the next special day."

She didn't phrase it like a question but paused anyway, as if I would respond. My thoughts rested on the small Christmases and birthdays that Mum used to throw me, I wished I'd intentionally enjoyed them more. Would I remember Ēostre celebrations if we'd stayed together?

"Do all races celebrate the same days?" I asked, stepping to the side briefly as a line of people ran after each other.

"We find our own meanings," she said, raising her mug to someone nearby, "but isn't it just nice to make something special of the everyday?"

Perhaps because of the closeness of the council chamber, I quickly began to notice others waiting a polite distance away. They were close enough for me to know they waited for one of us, but not familiar enough to be for me.

Thinking of the little opportunity I'd had over the past weeks, the words ran from my mouth. "Am I allowed to know if there's been any news about Mr Wilkins?"

Enid's hand raised as if to place it comfortingly on my shoulder, only she left it poised above me. "It's looking positive. We've been working on a new agreement, communications are just slow at the moment. We're all here if you need support, though." One of those waiting took another step but Enid took the time to smile and make sure I was okay, before greeting the closest person.

As my attention shifted, two or three others that had been talking or laughing began to head towards the valley. I took that as my cue about the time and finished my drink. Unsure what the layout would be, I made my way to refill my cup before finding Áine. The warmth from the fruity drink let me know it was probably fermented, but I let it burn away my apprehension about the amount of strangers around.

"Morgan, hurry!" I heard Ruari call, and I looked around to find them. They stood to the side of the central tunnel back out to the valley, many others waited too. Emer and Ruari had been sprayed with paint, their cheeks covered in ochre freckles and dark green vines that came to life across their faces.

"Wow, looks like you've been having fun already!" I said as I walked over. They pulled silly faces, exhibiting more of their face-paint whilst Emer stammered, her accent thickening in her excitement.

"It was to be thrown away. There's music!"

Áine clarified, "It's what they used to paint the walls. It'll wash off. Hungry?"

We traced the steps of the crowd as the music began to get louder again. I turned back to the girls. "Do either of you play?"

Emer stuck out her lip and gave Áine a glance before shaking her head. Áine smiled and pulled her sister in for a quick side hug. "Oh, you still might. Ruari could play the flute well when she actually practised." Their sister stuck out her tongue in response.

The rock opened up around us and twilight descended in its place. Winter clung to the edges of the fading light, where it was last to feel spring's arrival. Clouds passed slowly, revealing the occasional early star. Further away from the cave systems, musicians and performers had crowds around them as others skipped to the rhythm. We came to a natural pause, where I took the opportunity to look at some of the faces around us.

In our mornings helping, I'd met a few of them and seen more on the way to do their own work. Áine waved when a couple called a greeting.

"I think there's roasted dishes over there," she said. "That looks like raw food..."

People laughed and chatted as paths between them led to tables of food and drink. Not far from there sat a small pile of naturally coloured candles, their intricately woven carvings catching the fading light. At the heart of the festivities stood the bones of a proud bonfire and, as the sun dissolved, it was lit to an escalating cheer. People gathered around the catching flames, faces revealing the hope their springtime belief gave them. In that moment, the drums and string instruments renewed their vigour, and couples and families joined hands to commence the dance.

"Oh, there's someone I want you to meet! She arrived yesterday!" I was pulled from my watch, over to a woman standing by one of the food tables. She looked about ten years older than I was and cautious when we approached. Her brown hair was twisted back into an elegant crossed bun whilst the collar of her coat stood tall.

"Hello again," Áine called. "Morgan... this is your second cousin, Hazel. Your dad's father had a sister. When I heard she was visiting for Ēostre, I just had to introduce you. Her side of the family was given a gate further north."

Hazel looked me over and, unexpectedly, drew me into a light hug. "I can't believe Peredur had a daughter too, another gatekeeper in the family at that. Your father helped guide me when I was a girl, but he eventually stopped coming to our gatherings." She paused, taking in my unspoken question. "My grandmother is quite... traditional... and I believe your mother is from this world?"

I nodded, taking another mouthful of drink to clear the sticky feeling my throat had. Áine asked Ruari to get candles from a nearby stack.

"Some still believe our lineage needs to be kept pure..."

"Your parents didn't keep in contact?"

"For a while." She nodded. "It was hard for my mother when my father was injured, and they retired to Falias. They were able to look after my grandmother there too."

I stumbled over how to ask about their safety when Ruari returned, candles cradled in her arm, and handed one to each of us. The flames from the bonfire were dancing higher, and families started to move forward to carefully light their candles. Some of the candles were carried around, each one a work of art, though many others were placed on a makeshift altar adorned with fresh flowers and offerings of gratitude.

"Come on, then," Áine said to the girls when a space opened up. "What do you hope the new year will bring?"

Hazel and I stepped up behind them. She briefly invited me to go ahead of her before she said, "They signify the renewed energy, a reminder that it's all a cycle, even in the darkest times."

I didn't feel lighter. I could see how important the sentiment was to them at that time, but I had to fight an overwhelming urge to throw the candle in and watch it all waste away. I tipped the wick into a nearby flame trying not to think about it much more.

As far as I knew, they were still nursing their first mugs of mead, but I took the chance to step away and found a nearby barrel. After melting a little wax onto the table, I planted my candle alongside the cask and refilled my drink. My face was already pleasantly numbed against the night. I wanted to relax and let the warmth in my chest hold back my doubts for another night.

Shouts of joy joined the song as children ran about gleefully, their faces painted with flowers and spirals. When I returned, Emer was pulling Ruari into line and Drust had joined Áine and Hazel in conversation. The girls raced along with the others, finding district members handing out the flower crowns. As the night wore on, the dance became a whirl of spinning bodies and swirling skirts, feet tapping to the rhythm of the music.

"Will it all be back to work as normal tomorrow?" I asked Drust. He'd already refilled his cup too and had eyed a particularly raucous group on his way back.

"There's a day's grace or so. Some might find friends to change duties with them, but the day after will probably be normal. Don't worry, I won't ask too much of you." I didn't think it would matter anyway, if anything, his reactions only made it more difficult to listen to the world around me.

"How much 'grace' do I have?"

"Before what?" He glanced at me. Áine and Hazel were intent on their own conversation, and an odd laugh broke from my roommate.

"Before I'm asked to leave and left to the shadow." I avoided his look and watched Áine gesture a dance invitation to Hazel. One side of Hazel's mouth raised in a smile, and Áine left their mugs on the ground near our feet and twisted into the dance.

He lowered his voice, "Morgan, I don't follow the Seelie blindly. My interests align with theirs, but I follow my own conscience. If our instincts can bring us together, why would we leave you to die?"

It helped in that moment and added to the glow I felt.

"What were you worried Áine had told me before?"

He nodded his head away from the crowd in a where-it's-quieter motion. We left the relative warmth of the bonfire, and the current musicians grew quieter as those around us thinned. I felt so comfortably numb that I didn't care if we passed the ward's edge.

Drust looked around, his normally controlled expression departed. "This okay? It's not something I like to talk about really, not that it stops people from judging anyway." I met his gaze and nodded without really looking around. I could still make out the celebration in the distance, and the intermittent lanterns gave us enough light to make each other out, but we were still detached. His eyes relaxed in a way I hadn't seen yet, his dark eyebrows straightened into open regard. He suddenly cleared his throat and took off his jacket, draping it over the grass and offering me the first place.

I tilted my chin, unable to hide a small smile. Even if it meant grass stains, I was careful not to take up more than half of his coat, consciously arranging myself. I knew I shouldn't care really, but my blood fluttered when he sat facing me, arm resting on one raised knee. I finished the rest of my cup, hoping that sip to be the miraculous, steadying sip, and kept hold of the empty mug.

"My family," he began after finishing his own, "my blood family have done some questionable things, lied, corrupted, all but committed the treason themselves, but as I was a baby when my mother and grandfather were killed, I was offered to a barren couple since my father wasn't around. I don't know what I'd do without them." After a moment's pause, I wondered if his adoptive parents' situation was so hopeless that any consolation would be useless, but he cleared his throat and continued. "There are those who believe the corruption is in my blood, that I've got some innate allegiance to the Unseelie. People don't recognise me but... they know the name. Sometimes I think I feel it, a deep selfishness, but I've worked so hard to get where I am on my own merit. People who doubt me will always believe I'm part of some grand plan.

"When the council first asked me to help you, I wondered if they were setting me up to fail"—his eyes held mine—"but I've seen you work with the old magic, and everything I've learnt in my work tells me that you can reach what the Unseelie want... if that's what you want."

I wanted to steer us back, the conversation was getting uncomfortably close to the what-ifs that shadowed me. "What drew you into your work?" I sat a little taller, adjusting the recline I'd fallen into. The celebration continued a comfortable distance away, as if I'd found a solitary contemplation place, but we'd found it together.

"Well, it's a science really, a tool, and learning more about it can only give us progress. And we like to celebrate that." He inclined his head, just for a moment, eyes focused on me in the same way they had when we'd first met. "Do you know what else we celebrate on Ēostre?"

"Are you just giving me a line?" I smiled, willing my breath to come back. He raised his eyebrow at the same time a smirk hovered around his lips.

Leaning forward and lowering his voice as if giving me a secret, I barely caught his next words. "Can I kiss you?"

I wondered if my response would've been different if the mead hadn't softened the edges of my world. I didn't think about the situation these people had been put through, I didn't think about trying to channel whatever gift it was that I'd supposedly got from my father, I didn't think about leaving. Casually mirroring him as he drew closer, I nodded. My heart thundered.

Soft. Hot. Cautious. It was a caress, and it sent sparks among my butterflies. All I wanted was sensation, to let go of my mind but still have something to hold on to. I kissed back, and his mouth became firmer, more resolute. His hand came to the back of my neck, holding me close. My other senses dulled even further, the warmth from the alcohol spread throughout my limbs as my skin tingled in delight.

I guided my lips to his scarcely bristled jaw for a breath, to bring my body in, to press my chest closer to his. He didn't let go, trailing his kiss down to reach my throat. When we found each other again, hands found arms, waists, exploring. The music in the distance seemed to fade, becoming a hum in the background. I didn't care if everyone celebrated all night or became something quieter. I didn't care if anyone were to walk by, seeking their own place. I didn't care if someone thought it was wrong.

Taking my confidence from his embrace, I fell back onto one elbow, my clothes tickled as much as the grass. He retreated to a hand-span away, checking I was okay before joining me. I was selfish and, in my mind, he was too.

Chapter
Fourteen

The days began to blur together after that. I learnt. I worked. I tried to forget what was outside, which was difficult when that was where I felt most free. The weeks warmed, like the colours of the flowers that popped up in the valley. Snowdrops and daffodils turned into bluebells and poppies.

I continued through the routine that grew for the hours I got to explore the cave systems. There were layers of living, and it somehow suited the society that I had found myself in. After a collection of community caverns, it opened up into a network of residences. I couldn't work out how it might have looked from the woods but the more I thought about the outside, the more it felt like I was haunting a tomb. Regardless, I hadn't come across a perimeter guard yet, and I thought asking about how far I was allowed to walk might result in shorter walks. Maybe I had been wandering a little far, but I hadn't found any danger either.

After long stretches of people going about their daily chores, socialising or working, there was another layer of people doing the same thing outside the residential area, and then empty tunnels. When I first ventured into the darkness, the light from my lantern dancing on the rugged walls unnerved me, I kept expecting figures to jump out at me. Occasionally, other lanterns announced someone else nearby, often they were carrying mosses or old branches back.

Pelthas' chambers unfurled before me like chapters in an ancient tome. Patterns of lichen clung to the stone like living tapestries and stalactites hung like chandeliers from the ceiling, their slow, patient growth a reminder of the millenniums that had passed here. The air was cool and tinged with earthiness.

Amidst the shadows, I came across a few relics. Not unlike the carvings at the entrance, I found weathered knots etched into the rock. As I looked at them, the light revealed a recessed statue at its heart, its intricate design faded but still spoke of craftsmanship. I'd traced the lines with my fingers and wondered which of the Seelie legends it had been.

Further in still, along a winding passageway, I encountered chambers with long-forgotten fragments of another life. A bronze-coloured torc, its once-polished surface now patinated with age. Rings and a knife haft adorned with dust filled plaits. Intricately carved bone. Whispered stories.

Many of the carved pathways I walked looked similar and were only distinguished by collapsed rocks or cracks of different coloured stone when the coloured symbols ran out. I began to tell by the light or mossy density how close to the outside I was and listened to when I needed to head back along the stony coast.

The weight of the community spirit still felt so exhausting that only after keeping my head down with my assigned task did I look up to observe others. When I was a comfortable distance away, I remembered some of my own substance. I felt that Áine wanted to care for me like one of her sisters, but that attention was more responsibly spent on her girls. Ruari and Emer had begun their younger commitments again; Emer stayed behind at our communal meeting space for class of some kind and Ruari restarted her training in tailoring, seemingly the next step in settling their people. I might have felt differently about what I needed if I had the open road ahead of me. I thought I might feel clearer when Eoghan arrived. At first, I wanted to talk to him about my position and just hear the voice of the outsider, but the longer it took for him to visit, the deeper my doubts grew about why I was there.

I was overlooking the assembly plaza when Áine found me, the man I'd wanted to see three months ago in her stride. The opening I stood on acted like a balcony, closest to the fissure that lit the chasm. Áine and Eoghan passed a group that were whittling cups and bowls, exchanging conversation in grunts. I'd grown used to the different races that made up Pelthas, but I was still often reminded to be careful about my body language.

"There you are," Áine said cheerfully. "Look who's arrived!"

"I saw you coming." I smiled back, indicating over the ledge my arms rested upon, and greeted Eoghan. "I hope it hasn't been too bad in the outside world."

Áine turned and waved as she left.

Eoghan gave me an apprehensive look as he made the rest of his way over to me. "I'm afraid if you're asking that, you might have been keeping your head in the ground."

The irony wasn't lost on me. All I'd wanted these past months was to get my head out of the ground. "Has it been that bad?"

He gave a grim nod, eyes cast down when he replied, "It appears the Unseelie have stepped up their attacks. I believe another gate was lost based on what communication I've had, they must be getting desperate."

"My father's?"

"Still safe, and I'd hope even the council would tell you otherwise if that were the case. Oona has been able to rally some of her pack to help."

I didn't hear much from the council. They checked in when they saw me but whatever discussions they kept saying we needed never seemed to be as important as the next matter that came up. I wanted to be in the know, aware of the little details, but every time I tried to ask other questions, guilt clawed its way up my throat, preventing me. They were organising a refugee camp and liaising with other sites, caring for an entire city in their guardianship. Who was I to ask for their attention?

"Is it strange to be back?" I asked. During my time, I'd discovered Eoghan used to be a member of the council and given his confidence in his decision to be courtless, I hadn't been surprised. He knew how the system worked.

"It's far from what I used to know back home in Falias. Despite the harrowing situation, there's a part of me that's intrigued. I've read about Pelthas so often, the scholar in me can't help but be curious."

There was just a breath of quiet before the look I knew so well surfaced, familiar concern creasing his forehead. "And what about you? Are you settling in? Your vehicle is still safe, I passed it on the way in."

My way out. I felt for Rosie's key, still in my pocket, along with the brass shapes of my father's key that I knew so well now. I'd only been able to hope it would still be there and a little of my uncertainty lifted at Eoghan's words. Although I'd picked up a passing grasp of Sindaric, he spoke in English.

There were numerous other languages in the caverns that I just didn't encounter often enough to learn. Whilst I'd been here, I was either fervently welcomed to the point I doubted their sincerity or ignored. It made me miss the life I'd had before my mother passed. I missed her unwavering acceptance. There were exceptions of course. Áine, Drust, some on the council, remained realistic with me, but was that just because anything they were expecting from me was overdue?

"I don't know," I said finally. "I know the situation can't be helped, and I know I'm lucky to have somewhere safe, but I was backed into this too." I watched the figures below, working, living, even though they'd escaped war, what else could they do? "How long are you here for?"

"I don't think this is the life many of them would pick." He rested his bones against the rock, both hands on his cane. "I can stay as long as I want to. The council has concluded that Lunete's foretelling must have either been mistaken or, at the very least, not about me."

"So you're free to choose where you live?" I meant it as a happy statement, but he inclined his head.

"In a sense. It's been quite strange seeing ghosts from my past. Lovely too, catching up with some of them. But I think I'm too old to be uprooted now. I'm happy with my little home. I just had to give it a go, like you here."

"Who's saying that?" I felt a little shame, annoyed at my response. Hadn't I done everything I was asked to do so far?

"I meant no insult, only that if you need help, you need just ask."

I shifted, half unsure how to respond, half inclined to let the comment pass as if I hadn't heard it. A figure that I made out to be Áine left from the direction of the carved stairs, her chestnut hair striking even from the bun she wore. She weaved between the groups, casually pausing and greeting people as she passed. She stopped when she reached a space outside the cavern square.

"I'm not sure what I've done to upset Oona." I turned back to him as he looked back to me as well.

"You've seen her?"

"Mostly from a distance. She didn't like it when I tried to say hello."

Eoghan was quiet for a second before clearing his throat. "I'm sure lots of things have changed around here recently. No one can say for certain, she's on high alert."

There was something in the way he glanced away that made me doubt what Eoghan meant. I didn't want to think like that— like he was hiding things from me too. I'd waited patiently to talk to someone whose advice I thought I could listen to. Without him, I was closer to just existing for a little while and trying life again later.

"No updates on what the Unseelie might be doing?" he asked.

I shook my head, looking back out across the layers of caves, and thought it was curious that he thought I might have more information on that. "Not that I've heard. Áine tells me that a lot of their resources are put into protection at the moment, but much of their library had to stay behind of course, so that makes it especially difficult to research their theories. What about you? Any ideas?"

I found myself trying to find her again in the thinning crowd below. She wasn't in the space from before but hadn't gone far. She walked with another figure, towards one of the dining spaces. The shape and stride of her companion was familiar. I caught myself searching for his outline occasionally. I also knew Áine hadn't mentioned that they were on another task together. I was much too far away to see their expressions or make out what they were talking about. Although I had more reason to see Drust by then, we still only checked in for practice and even that was less than it had been. He was quiet about his parents, but I gathered he'd heard from all the camps now. They were missing in Falias.

I had little success, or interest, in the simplest manipulation anyway. I didn't know how to be a gatekeeper and, if I thought about committing to this one path, the lives I left unlived crowded my mind. Had Mum taken me away to let me pick a different life?

"It makes sense that they've stepped up their efforts; they either get more gates or more reaction." Eoghan looked around casually as if checking for any listeners. "The Seelie have fought, but the time disturbance has inhibited their ability to travel too. They have no way of bridging worlds to the right time. They can plan all they like but they must wait for the Unseelie to act."

It should have had more impact on me than it did. "That's comforting."

"I tell you these things to remind you of your choices, Morgan. You can still live outside of all this, but it can be a good life if you let it."

I'd only wanted to get to know the other side of me, another piece of myself. Some of Mum's stories had felt a little too real when I was growing up and the influences on my life had led me here. But I couldn't help but feel it was still an act. In that moment, I asked myself if I thought I would survive outside all this, and wondered how long I would stay in Pelthas because of that?

Chapter
Fifteen

"Can we talk a moment?"

Cold shot through my spine as I immediately thought of our night together a couple of months ago. Drust's eyebrows straightened in concern. I was still turning up to our sessions, and we were most recently practising physical control, but controlling what was outside of us remained out of reach for me.

"Of course," I said, knowing it wouldn't be our normal exchange of ideas and smirked quips.

"Things can get chaotic in the caverns," he said as we began slowly walking back, it had warmed up quickly this year and invited an abundance of flower heads to appear in the valley. Just like Ēostre was a celebration for the Seelie, Litha was coming around just as quickly as the last festival. "Sometimes it can feel like everyone expects you to know your role, especially when it's something whole families get involved with."

"I can't imagine people coming together like this from the town I came from. Was it the same back in Falias? Big celebrations?"

He nodded. "Generally, however many days the celebration is, we'll have the same to prepare. The cities don't run themselves, but it gives people something to look forward to."

There had still been no word about his parents. Every few weeks he postponed our sessions to travel to another camp. He told me one afternoon that it was in case they were among the injured. I selfishly wanted to travel with him, if only to see more, but it felt like I would be asking to join him on a pilgrimage. I didn't know how he found the energy to hope and I tried to give him a space to see that.

"What does your family normally help to prepare?"

"When they worked, they were in the Second Council, which is normally food. Priority number one, isn't it? Making sure everyone has food." It should be, I thought in response, thinking of the differences between them-and-us and just-us. He moved back in conversation. "I meant it can get crazy in the enclosed sense too. I realise that's probably something you've never done before. It can feel like it's pressing in on me sometimes."

Like I'd suspected this conversation was something else, I knew it was also an invitation. A depth echoed back at me. It said I know, I've been there, but I'm here if it's too much. I felt pieces of me quicken and still in tandem, like I couldn't breathe. The polite span of time for a response passed quickly, and although I couldn't help but think of the expectation to manage it from my past, I was tempted. To have company in the dark.

The part of me that quickened arrived at panic and wanted to leave our conversation at that. What did it matter if I wasn't planning to stay here anyway?

"It is what it is, at least you know the truth about why I'm still turning up to our sessions." I indicated around us to the open air and the late afternoon day.

"What about your walks past Pelthas?," he said, "I'm not sure if we know where some of those passages go. Found anything interesting?"

"It's been thousands of years here. I'd be surprised if I did find anything. There's only so far I can go whilst it's still light, don't really fancy going at night either." I marked my way when I explored. There were often colour differences in the rock, but I'd only found something interesting once— stratum that almost glowed at the time of day I'd found it, the quartz layer had formed a wave around the cavern.

I couldn't stop my mind turning back to the meetings we'd had with the council. Was this a situation where what we talked about would be fed back? We'd learnt so little about what the Unseelie were doing, and I was beginning to loathe the fact that I'd had to make a choice in the first place. If Mum had known about any of this, did she regret not talking about any of it? It was so different from our world at Joanne's antique shop, it could've been from a different life already. My chest ached a little, remembering the strawberry plants in the little yard to the side.

He turned his head to look at me as we slowed, nearing the entrance. It was quiet. "It can be disheartening, when all I've ever done is try to serve the council, some people still only see me for what my mother's and grandfather's actions were. I believe in what the Seelie do though, and in return I choose how I want to live." I met his gaze and even as I kept my breathing natural, I could see what he might be doing.

"But people will think what they will." He shrugged slowly. "What's important is how I feel about it and whether I truly believe I can follow my own judgement."

His words echoed in my head as I examined them one at a time. Part of me heard all these words of concern, whilst another part wanted to retreat further into the silence, angry at the disturbance. They weren't worried about Drust's judgement. Were they worried about my judgement? "And I guess I shouldn't be trusting my judgement at the moment? Has this come from Áine?"

"That's not—"

Pain unexpectedly sprouted up my throat. It urged me to broach the night I'd told myself not to bring up. "Was my judgement flawed on Ēostre?" All things considered, life overturned, I did think I'd been managing. There was a brief moment when I considered the contrast in our cultures, but I had hoped that Drust and Áine would at least see it from my eyes.

"You tell me," he said quietly, expression hardening.

I gripped my coat around me, not knowing how to respond but getting more frustrated the longer the silence grew. "I'm fine, and if Áine asked you to speak to me, she should know she can speak to me herself. Better yet, see the effort I'm putting in to help with whatever I can."

I turned to head back inside when he said after me, "We see you withdrawing. She has tried, and I hate to use that as a point, but if you haven't noticed, that might be worth examining too."

The thorns clung to me. I hoped I had enough self-awareness to notice if darkness draped over my thoughts, but I wouldn't have admitted it in that moment even if I had recognised it.

Chapter
Sixteen

I had been curious about the white-haired sister since she'd spoken to me at our arrival. The pieces I'd collected about her from casual conversation made her feel all the more otherworldly. No matter how difficult it was to speak to some members of the council, the sisters simply disappeared into their own administration. She found me when I'd been assigned sweeping duty. Out of the basic jobs I'd been given, it was the one I minded least. It was inevitable that mud was tracked in through the tunnels, but I didn't mind when I went exploring by myself anyway.

"You must know most of the city by now." Her voice came from behind me. I rested the brush against my hip as I turned to face her and her uniformed protection. Many faces that surrounded the council seemed familiar now and this officer was one of them. She had been among one of the first groups sent to secure Pelthas.

"It's hard to tell honestly. I haven't had any way to map myself since arriving. Have you come to join me?" I put on a smile and inclined my head in what I hoped was respect— I hadn't been told otherwise. My blood ran with unease. They hadn't looked for me since I'd arrived.

She smiled, her eyes shifting beyond their cloud whilst seemingly watching me. "In a sense. I'm surprised you haven't yet sought out the place of the first gate, but I'd be honoured to show you if you'd like."

Her invitation surprised me, and I didn't know how to respond for a few seconds. Had I been allowed to look for that? "Was I supposed to be finding it? That sounds like something I shouldn't refuse."

"We can drop that off along the way," she said, referring to the broom I still held. As we walked, I noticed a respectful reverence from the people around her. The curtsies and bows that didn't have a place in the world I came from, the offerings of whatever these people had to spare, the trust and allegiance.

Just once she approached a group at the side and spoke very quietly with them. It didn't come across for show and, along with other passing folk, I knew to stay behind with Dairíne, Lunete's guard.

"Sometimes her feelings have real impact. I believe some of her struggle comes from knowing which ones to follow," she said when we waited.

Lunete was back over before I had time to respond, and after continuing, the familiar dwindling of people was a relief as we left the more populated areas. We walked in the lower levels of the city, past the places that others lived and worked. The further we went, a hum I hadn't noticed before grew louder. There was no sound, only a sort of reverberation in the air, but it was insistent, and I didn't know how I hadn't noticed it before.

"Can you feel this up in the city?" I asked.

"Sometimes." Lunete looked around the rock. "Other times it becomes necessary for me to tune into what is important."

"There are other energies here, then?" We walked into a passage I hadn't seen before, its lanterns spaced further out than those in the levels above. A glistening line in the rock's strata led us further down before disappearing completely when we reached a few roughly hewn steps. I looked at Dairíne briefly before following, and she nodded before making a point of resting behind us.

"The forces that we're all able to tap into are not so different," Lunete said as she continued down the steps towards a gentle glow. "It's said that we were granted these gifts from the gods of our homeland, what you call Northern Europe now. After our ancestors arrived in Inis Fáil, they were eventually found and invaded by Unseelie Fomorians, and that was when we were driven to Albios for the first time."

As we drew closer to the glow, it formed into a large underground pool. Walled by ancient rock that looked as if it had always been one piece, it spanned from one side of the cavern to the other, the radiance seemingly coming from the water itself. Lunete gave me a moment to take it in, the surface mirror-still whilst there was only a trickle that whispered around us.

"Despite having to leave our records behind... I can tell you we never found our original homeland again."

"What d'you think happened?" I asked quietly, aware of the respect I should show. Even though the carvings along the base of the waist-high wall had mostly worn away, I felt like they had once been symbols of tribute.

"Either everyone left together, scattered themselves like dandelion seed or all died somehow. Like other family traits, gifts like yours and mine are believed to be closer to those of our forebears, but they are given unpredictably. Oh, there are variations, I believe..." She looked to me and started again. "We purposefully haven't told the people the location here, and there's a reason they're not all converging here without the council saying anything."

I could only think that this was the place she'd previously said had become the first gate and that there was a reason she'd brought me here. Their belief that I held a particular strand of my father's gift sat heavily at the back of my mind.

"I don't know what to do here," I said after a moment's pause. There wouldn't be a better time to let them see my concerns. My thoughts began to feel as complicated as the task they might ask of me. "I can't even work it out for myself, let alone do something for the greater good."

Around us, the rock strata were surprisingly similar to the rest of Pelthas. It was the plant life that drew my focus afterwards. Among the blanched mosses, simple leaves reached towards the edge of the pool. They were wide and equally pale as if soaking up whatever was radiating from its surface.

"It would be unwise to ask you to do anything here. I mean no disrespect when I say I doubt you'd have any control over where we'd go and, if we were to reach Falias, we would walk straight into the Unseelie." I felt no sting from her words, they were gentle and true. She offered a small smile as she continued. "I find the best way to approach what we do is to treat it like something wild. Patience and learning help us build trust in what we can each do. How you've decided to treat it, the time you get to know it, should dilute your fear in what it might do. I hope this isn't too obscure."

I knew what she was trying to express, but I wasn't sure if I wanted to know it. What if I never tried to invoke these energies again? There was a chance the shadow wouldn't be flagged down again at all. "I don't know what I'm doing here. I'm not contributing to anything."

She reached for my hand, her aim precise. "I've lived in the shadow of the Unseelie all my life, and they don't stop. It is greed. They simply do not see the cost it has on the rest of us."

"Can I ask if the council knows who betrayed your family?" It was out before I really had time to think about what I was asking and felt I should add some context. "I know Eoghan was originally thought to be the threat..."

"I have my suspicions." She paused. "When my father pushed the Unseelie back all those years ago, he was particularly thorough, and I believe these are the ripples of his reaction. I was a girl when I saw my brother's future, but through my actions and my father's ideas of propriety, I pushed him into it instead. I was playing their game but I didn't know the rules. We can't be anything other than who we are against the Unseelie's ruthlessness."

"Would you do anything differently?"

"I wouldn't assume to jump on the first meaning I found," she said, her expression made pensive by the direction of her eyes. "Sometimes I find that the hardest part about it all was that I lost my big brother, even when some say he was always headed that direction. But we will never know that."

As she spoke, I was reminded of my own family and suddenly knew it wouldn't have made a difference if Mum and I had stayed. I still would've ended up in this city, or possibly dead alongside my father, helping others escape. Perhaps then, I could leave now and it wouldn't make any difference either. My father's key rested comfortably in my pocket.

"I'm sorry your family's had to go through something like this," I said, not wanting to let it pass without comment.

"Likewise," she said gently. "Everyone will encounter something. All we can do is have empathy and remember that even understanding is an influence in this world. We affect each other's lives; we can't escape that, so what impact would you rather have?"

I didn't want to have any influence. The idea that it wouldn't matter if I left anyway took root, I should take any chance I had. I wondered whether I was beginning to lose the feeling of imminent threat in the caverns. Absently, my hand found its way to my pocket, outlining the brass pattern I knew so well.

Lunete tilted her head suddenly and my blood slowed at the possibility she would claim it as a Seelie possession.

"Did you bring anything here that wasn't yours? Perhaps find something along the way?"

"I didn't steal anything if that's what you mean." My tone was sharper than I meant it to be, but it was mine. They laid claim to the gate that sat in my father's house. I felt like I was allowed to keep the small personal things that said something to me. I deliberately stilled my hand, the fear hardening in my blood.

"It's not an accusation... I can just hear... You should know there have been reports of nearby Unseelie from our protective divisions. Your link with the old magics must be worth their efforts," she said. "We often think the people have enough to manage when some families won't be the same again, but these are manipulative forces, and it would be prudent for you to be careful."

Having been interested in where this conversation was going before, I was suddenly disheartened by the implication and repeated advice. I thought I might learn something that afternoon, but I felt more alone. I'd left what I knew behind me, harmonised as well as knew how, and felt like I was trying to reach impossible forces. I didn't have the capacity to think about what they thought I should be doing.

"I have been careful." Circling thoughts began to overflow in an angry torrent. "I've tried to be useful. And I've gone with every direction I've been given. But I'm getting tired of not knowing what it's all for. How much of my life should I be willing to waste when I didn't ask to be in this situation? I don't know what my life is supposed to be yet, but the only other option I seemingly have is the shadows out there." Was that where I headed anyway, trapped in these ancient caverns? I was in the dark anyway.

"We just want you to be safe." Lunete's head was tilted, her hand caught between us when I hadn't noticed it leave me.

"Why? What is it I'm supposed to do?"

"Trust yourself. When that becomes clear, I'm sure you'll have preferred to have more time."

The longer I stayed here, the less comforting this became. I wanted to leave.

I turned, knowing that if I didn't leave and try to avoid all this, this feeling would just get worse and worse. I knew Rosie was still within walking distance. I would have to flag someone down to jump start her battery, but I could still leave this all behind me. I strode back the way I remembered, hoping I wasn't leaving anything I needed behind in my backpack. I thought about Áine and her sisters but knew they had each other. They would be happy to have their space back anyway.

Briefly looking over my shoulder as I headed into the main cavern, I realised no one was following me. I knew I could probably move quicker than Lunete, and Dairíne couldn't leave Lunete. They would have to find others and that took a little time. In any case, no one had told me they would follow, and I wondered if I was just being silly. I'd forgotten the depths the shadow could make me feel.

In the tunnels back out, I checked my pockets, knowing my keys hadn't moved. I wanted to feel their comfort anyway. I'd left my phone behind, the battery long since dead. I could get another cheap one if it meant not explaining myself to anyone else, and I could live with what was in my van.

Chapter
Seventeen

I knew which direction we'd arrived in relation to the communal cavern. I didn't stop to look back at the arched entrances in the rock behind me and followed the lanterns back out. The air felt the same as that in the valley, if a little sweeter for the knowledge of what I was doing. I couldn't turn around now, or I'd never get myself this far again.

It was still afternoon, though only a small amount of light made its way into the tunnels. I noticed each difference on the way out, the lighter shade of rock around me, the tufts of life along the pathway, the damper air. By the time I reached the familiar clearing, I'd nearly turned back three times, the memory of the attack when we'd arrived still in my periphery. I remained cautious but it was brighter than I'd expected, as if my disposition added to the lightness. The border of the woods flattened at one point and led away in the direction I vaguely remembered us coming.

The clearing held the same quiet as the valley, breeze and birdsong. I hoped to be able to hear a road, one that I hadn't noticed on the way in, but only discerned how empty it was out there. I felt my breath deepen, in anticipation of meeting a patrol or someone trying to get in. I didn't wait around. Happy to follow my instincts, I immediately headed into the ferns. Branches and leaves from past years carpeted the woods, but between the gaps of the trees, delicate flowers of lilac and periwinkle emerged from patches of their own foliage.

It was still light enough for me to take the path faster than I normally would have, and I hopped over the occasional fallen bough, trying to remain alert to what was around me. I didn't know what else to expect, from the reports that circulated in the caverns. Anyone would have expected an attack by now.

I didn't know which direction I headed in. Through the leaves above, the overcast sky hid any clues given from the sun. When the clouds began to absorb the light, growing heavy, I slowed my pace. I only had the memory of how long we'd walked before to guide me, and I wasn't even too confident in that. When we arrived just over a few months ago, there had been a river we stopped at along the way where Áine had refilled her water. Much of the forest had filled out, enjoying the summer, transforming it, and I began to doubt my direction when I finally heard water. I didn't think it was far to my van from that point. Finding my way down the stair-like roots, I gave another glance around the trees to check for any followers before stepping down onto the stony bank for a drink.

The water ran swiftly, vibrant weeds at the bottom snapped in the rush. I hadn't carried a bottle with me and hadn't thought to trade for one of their flasks. Crouching down, I let the water overflow the cup of my hands and drained it. Repeating the process, I knew I needed to get on the road soon. I'd have little hope of finding anything at all if any more light faded above me.

I moved to stand, thinking about how certain I was in my direction, when the world shimmered around me.

I held myself up against the air, hands spread, wondering if I was more dehydrated than I thought. It wasn't dizziness—the air swayed as if a piece of glass moved around me. My focus escaped with it, but the surrounding colours seemed to call me back with their vibrancy. Standing still for a moment, I tried to get my thoughts together enough to decide if I could just keep going. I felt my focus jumping, any movement around me intensified as if held under water. My heartbeat moved in time with every leaf flutter or bird.

Was it possible for the Unseelie to lay sickness like a trap?

I took a deep breath, one of my hands flattened against the key in my pocket as I straightened. I'd been willing to simply let whatever was going to happen, happen, when I left a couple of hours ago. I tried to hold onto that feeling.

I peered over to the river briefly, justifying that I'd looked at the state of the water before drinking it. Rocks danced at the edge where it rippled into deeper shades of forest. Clear enough and fast enough.

But... running in the same direction I was going... away from the cave system that hid the first gate. Was it possible something had happened? Was that something the Seelie would have warned me about? I backed up against a tree, glad for its strength, even though I hadn't realised I'd moved.

The trickling of the water got louder, and, like everything else around me, the movement of its tide quickened and shifted. Aiming to start moving again, in hopes of finding something else to drink in my van, I found myself frozen instead.

I couldn't say how long I tried to focus on the folding water. I was just as aware of all the smaller movements that had distracted me moments ago. There was blackness— it couldn't have been long really because the remaining light was still holding on when I came to. It could have been an extended blink.

When I could distinguish what I was seeing again, I noticed that I was laying down. I mentally checked my body. I didn't feel any pain, and thought I still recognised my foot from my hand. After trying to move my hands to push myself up, I was reminded that only "moments" ago, I'd been frozen. I still couldn't move. The world went quiet. After ironically wondering if anyone might pass and how long it might be, I felt my panic set in.

It wasn't long before a shadow passed into view. My blood raced again. Had the darkness found me so quickly?

The longer I focused on it, the more it slowly sharpened into a straight figured woman. She was vaguely familiar, but I couldn't place her. Leaning over me, her eyebrow raised in an otherwise disinterested face. Long dark hair fell limp against her pallor. Her mouth moved, but I couldn't hear the words she was saying. She motioned to someone else outside my sight line, and a moment later, I felt pressure on my arms as someone helped me lean up. The blood pounding in my ears fell away enough for me to hear other people pacing behind me.

The woman knelt in front of me and, voice dampened, she said, "It will be okay."

She took my hand and then plunged it into the same river I'd just drunk from.

I don't fully trust my memories from the moments in between. One moment we were in the woods and the next, the trees had cleared. It could have been the same place in a different course of decisions. The land was still uncared for, but it looked as if it had been farmed up until recently.

As I slipped in and out of consciousness, it occurred to me that one of these blackouts could be it for me, and I wouldn't know. I could still see the dark-haired woman who'd spoken to me before. I tried to use her like an anchor when I awoke in between. I would make sure that she was still somewhere nearby. My arms were being held as I stumbled along behind her.

Every time my consciousness surfaced, I felt too dull to panic. I forced my eyes to move, to take in as much as I could, to remember it if I had to. I kept trying to raise my head, to look at who was beside me, to gain anything extra from our surroundings, to find anyone else, to chase away the numbness.

There were other people that moved in and out of my sight— those with predatory features and sharp teeth. Occasionally I could make out a burbled sentence between them, the tones extending like a bad recording. Some part of me clung to the possibility that Lunete had called the group to retrieve me but the more I saw of the landscape, the more I realised how far we had travelled. And I had no idea how to get back.

The farmland around us grew more shapes, some which could be nothing more than rubble or piles of charcoal. When whole buildings weaved before me, there were more figures, but none drew near enough for me to see them properly. The colour of the ground shifted from the less-trodden green to dirty paths of fitted stone. With no help from my unfocused eyes, I tried to concentrate on what I was hearing more. It was still as if I was underwater and, whilst I could understand a passing amount of Sindaric by that point, the words I heard were broadened further with accent.

At this point, I wondered if my numbness was a secret blessing and if any terror I was supposed to be feeling was also being suppressed. I watched but, inside, I knew I wouldn't be able to do anything with the coldness seeping into my limbs.

We eventually arrived somewhere, the walls rising up around my eyes. There were still other figures around, except they hurried past, and what I saw around my shoes seemed cleaner. We came to a stop at the entrance of a large room, the span of it disappearing past what I could see. Figures moved from a large object in the centre. Murmuring came to a stop, and the group's presence was enough to pause what was going on.

"My Lord, may I introduce the gatekeeper that your shade discovered?"

A disturbance stopped as soon as it started. Some of the peripheral spectators were keen to follow what was happening. One figure drew nearer. I could see that they were tall, and they stopped in front of the woman to my left— the one who had spoken to me before, seemingly the one who was in charge of this little group. They were slender and had dark skin like the prime sisters. He looked at me before leaning towards the woman and murmured something to her. I couldn't make out what was said, but I also couldn't hear any indication that the surrounding people had either.

The woman stepped back and her figure turned suddenly. Walking quickly, she entered my field of vision and, just as swiftly, raised a hand to those beside me. We all moved, heading back the way we'd come and reentered the dark halls. Through the coldness I felt and my mind's disconnection, I knew there was something obvious I was missing. It was only when I awoke again that the depth of my situation hit me.

Chapter
Eighteen

A female with long white hair stood in front of several other figures. Many were in similar outer layers, and many looked towards this woman's group. They communicated in the same language that the others that commanded.

"I fear that the Unseelie had a way of influencing Morgan." Her sound was light, her expression serious. "I had a sense once before and hoped she would be comfortable enough to let me help her. But Dairíne has also had some unsettling news." She indicated to another person, who stood.

"The shadow we've been looking for has been sighted, past the grove, towards the town. One group tried to ambush it but were left empty-handed. According to the timings, it's likely been circling Pelthas, possibly for a way in, possibly for Miss Woods."

A female with bright hair from behind the circle stood, pulling a dark-haired male up beside her. "If we may add, there have been further reports of Morgan crossing the protective line. If she was being influenced in some way, it was only a matter of waiting, keeping us distracted with small attacks. We would like to try and find her, with or without any help that can be spared."

"Was this a reliable report?" said the one who had spoken before.

"Yes—"

One of the figures in the circle, their grey hair pulled into a sphere, makes an odd sound. "The council member who was exiled on suspected treason does not count as reliable."

"Surely if she is this vital to the Unseelie's plans, we should be looking for her anyway."

"Among many that are vital to how they work, our priorities to everyone else have not changed. How do we know she didn't choose to leave? Were we holding her prisoner?"

Another figure adds their own tones. "I think stepping back is also worth the consideration and would like to preface this, prime sisters, by meaning no disrespect to your family. We know this creature is drawn to gatekeeper energy and is collecting it somehow, we also suspect its roots are in Albios. Is it possible that we might be able to get our people home by using it?"

There was some quiet after this figure stopped before the central woman, whose hair was wrapped around her head, restarted the talking. "I'm sure I speak for my sister too, Enid, when I say we will never turn away ideas that have our community at its heart. But we must advise that taking the life of the one who gave you life will never create something good."

More noise rose among the spectators, but the dark-haired male could be heard saying. "What they're not getting is that the Unseelie have a source of energy, and someone to channel it, so what else do they need?"

The woman with bright hair gave a grim smile, the top of her face lined. "Something to ignite it?"

"Well, it's like Eoghan theorised months ago... what if they already have that too?"

Chapter
Nineteen

I must have blacked out for good because when all of my senses woke, I was laying on a basic bench to the side of an unadorned room. I remembered the hallway. It took me a few minutes to piece my fragmented memory together, and, when I'd found the obvious pieces that I couldn't connect before, I knew I was with the Unseelie. I knew the figure in the hall had been T'sol, the shadow's summoner, tormentor to the families at Pelthas who'd lost everything.

Sitting up, I could see that there wasn't anybody in the room, but I knew better than to assume I was totally alone. Trying not to think about any possible scenarios, I made my way over to the door and tried the handle, fully expecting it to be locked. It turned under my hand. I paused and then slowly made a gap to see outside.

It wasn't quiet. The diversity in the hall was comparable to the caverns. But they all just seemed tired and empty. Past the odd ones walking through, I made out two sinewy figures at the end of the hall, dressed in simple leathers shaped into a makeshift uniform. From where I stood, I could make out the height of their antlers and angular shade of their jaws. Their standpoint made me think I was their responsibility and, wanting to think my situation through a little, I closed the door again just as gently.

Even if I was able to make it outside the hallway, I didn't know my way out. I didn't know my way back to the gate they had used, and I didn't know how I was supposed to react if anyone stopped me or tried to hurt me. I didn't know what else was in this place.

Casting back, my mind groped for its last substantial memory. I remembered the river, and wished I had asked more about my father's gift directly. I was aware of the real possibility that I might have helped transport us all, and felt acid creep up my throat at what that could mean. Could it happen again if I was able to find it?

It wasn't long before the door opened, and the same woman who'd spoken to me before entered with a glass of water. She inclined her head, dark hair swaying, when she saw I was sat on the thin mattress.

"Good morning." Her voice was low and quiet. She spoke Sindaric. I found myself leaning forward to listen. "How are you feeling? My name is Neasa."

"Hello..." I watched her, unsure about our dynamic. Though I'd heard many names since meeting these people, I was certain I hadn't heard the Seelie Council talk about her. She rested the glass on the table, the only other bit of furniture there, and remained where she was. Her eyes watched me as I watched her, her hand rested next to the glass as if steadying herself.

"These past couple of years have been trying for everyone. Re-establishing order is never easy, and we had nearly gone back to our original strategy." Then, after a pause, she said, "Can you understand me?"

I wondered suddenly if feigning misunderstanding would lead me to overhear more of what they were hoping to do. I knew I probably wouldn't be present when they discussed tactics though. Deciding it would only be a reason to distrust me if something slipped, I nodded slowly. "But then I left Pelthas?"

"But then we learnt that there were gate waters in use. It was a matter of security." Her expression was controlled. Then, as I felt myself reaching to say something that might help me get back, she continued. "We haven't been aware of you for very long, your gifts must still be tired from waking."

I thought back to my sessions with Drust, and the feelings of panic and entrapment rose again at how little we'd achieved. Would it go better for me here if they thought I could do more? All their specialities had been varied so far.

"Where were you going?"

In the space of a deep breath, I leant into every moment I'd felt closest to myself, reaching for when things had lined up. "Home," I said, reflecting her empty face. "I must have underestimated how much attention you had on it."

Her eyebrow raised but not enough to fill the blankness, "We might be able to help you back"—my heart thudded—"but we'd require something in return." The rush of blood made me feel dizzy.

"What would you need me to do?"

"What have the Seelie told you so far?"

I would have liked more time before this conversation to pull myself together, my head a little clearer, and found a little more by fidgeting. "About what?"

"Do you know how long this has gone on for? Why should one council have say over the other? We have lost just as much, if not more, and had to take control for *our* people." Though her jaw ticked, her voice remained steady. I thought about Áine and her sisters, Urien after he'd returned, hearing the news about his son. I thought of the kindness and empathy the Seelie treated each other with, and I swallowed.

"If I'm to be part of this," I said carefully, "that's not a decision I can make right now."

"It's not a decision"—a corner of her mouth raised, almost a smile—"you'll make your own way. There are opportunities here, you can pursue anything you'd like to do."

There was some vital piece about the courts' discord I was missing, but I knew I would give away too much away if I asked any questions. It was a situation that I obviously didn't know enough about. Instead, I tried "So I'm allowed to explore?" I hoped I'd be able to come to my own conclusions if I was allowed to look around.

For the first time, she looked around the room, then said, "I should think so, but T'sol would also like to meet you." She turned back to me. "You were so exhausted when we found you that I think it's best to stay in the nearby hallways for the time being. You might be feeling a little better now, but until you've given yourself time to recover, you'll feel tired quickly."

I took that to mean I'd be watched until that meeting and felt the discomfort of déjà vu. I'd been hidden under another wing until another council decided what to do with me.

Resolving to find the crux of what this was all about, I swallowed my resentment and tilted the lens I was looking through— seeing different things was what I wanted to be doing anyway.

"I'll take you to him tomorrow. Those you see with different coloured armbands outside can help if you need anything." Neasa turned to leave and, as I wanted to ask about going outside this building, I felt the shadow's weight on my desire to do anything.

She pulled the door closed again, and my head dropped back onto the wall by the bed. My focus drifted onto the situations I'd found myself in and which pathways had led here. Somehow it consumed my effort, and I didn't know how long I sat like that.

Afterwards, I would see how similar it felt to the times I'd been haunted when I was younger and, although I couldn't see a way out, I knew there was something I should have been doing.

Only when I shifted, finding a new arrangement for my muscles, did I think about getting up and investigating again. My senses lurched when I stood. My hand found the wall as I breathed through the desire to fall back down.

I had a vague awareness that I hadn't felt this bad before Neasa's visit. But I couldn't spare the energy to care whether it was her or the influence of the shadow in this place.

When I got to the door, the hallway outside didn't feel as busy as the first time, though there were still people moving around in groups, and others gently carrying things at the sides. I noticed the armbands she'd mentioned and, as I stood there, realised the armbanded were all going about specific tasks—

blue for water buckets, white for piles of folded clothing. The two guards in makeshift uniform had only shifted down the passage a few paces, and my eyes lingered on them as I slowly walked out into the hall. I hoped they'd been told I could look around too.

By the time I headed towards a mirroring corridor of polished wood and stone, I'd decided that my best chance was to simply walk by. After I passed, the ceiling rose into something grander, numerous doors were everything between open and closed before the only direction led down a set of stairs. I peered back the way I'd come, aware that I might not even find my way back to that room. At the same time, I saw that rather than stopping me from leaving, the guards were still about the same distance away from me, walking behind me. Like that then, I thought.

Below the small mezzanine, it grew busier again, more armbanded people, more guards, and seemingly, more public. Groups pressed close and moved in a familiar way. I realised they must be the families who had been left behind. There were families who had all received the same duty, those who were too young to work and had no choice but to follow their parents or siblings, or those who couldn't work and huddled in rags. I saw the same etchings of fatigue and hopelessness echoed in their faces. Among them, vicious-looking Aspects, like those I'd seen in the park, and bands that taunted the others against the walls.

In hopes of finding a way out, I was about to head down the stairs into the press of people when a hand closed over my arm, making me jump. One of the sinewy guards had drawn closer, their skull-like head tilted at me, their eyes vacant. They indicated back the way we'd come with a sharp antler. The same moment I thought I would refuse them, became the same time a cautious feeling about getting lost began to grow. It fogged my capacity to think about other ways of reacting, and I was filled with the feeling that I could always find my way out. Suddenly I just wanted my own space again. I headed back with them, feeling the closeness of a place to sit alone as it drew nearer and nearer.

• • • •

Occasionally the fog did lift. The days blurred, but I couldn't find the effort to care about whatever was going on here. On a clearer day, or perhaps I was intentionally released for a short while, Neasa visited again. She knocked and entered without waiting for my response. I'd been mostly left to my own company and the expectation of a visit had grown. A visit and an answer.

When I began to think about what she'd said last time, I didn't know if the lack of opportunity disappointed me at Pelthas. Although that offer and the Seelie's shattered reality were disconnected, I couldn't help but compare them. Hadn't I been seeking something of my own before all this? Back when my skin crawled with restlessness? If I stayed in the same place for too long, I couldn't help but wonder what the other experiences were. Why did she say it as if it was something the Seelie couldn't do?

"We have some time." She didn't enter much further than before and looked at me slouched against the wall. "Did you want some time to freshen up?"

I had barely moved, and as my thoughts pieced themselves together, I could feel the dried sweat on my skin, the barely touched food traces growing cotton in my mouth. I wanted to retreat back into the depths I'd just surfaced from.

"Come, it'll ease as you walk with me." She gave no indication of helping me out from the nest I'd surrounded myself with and I couldn't decide if that embarrassed me more or less.

Pain shot up my legs as I tried to untangle myself, the vertebrae of my back popping like ice. My thoughts were rusty, but I began to wonder how long I'd been sat, caught in that same cycle of thought. I could nearly grasp the bigger picture again. I hated to think about how much time I'd wasted and resolved to purposefully try. What else could I do?

Neasa only waited until I was moving before leaving again. Taking one big step, I followed into the hallways I should've explored by now. Though I couldn't be certain we hadn't gone downstairs when I'd first been brought here, I realised we were heading in a different direction when there were more stairs. It was the first time I'd gone further than my hallway without an entourage, and the further I walked with Neasa, the clearer my mind became.

From the time I'd been out on my own and that time falling into her step, I could see the same fear and exhaustion in these people. I could see the conditions they were subjected to from the state of their clothes and their gaunt figures. I noticed how small everyone in armbands tried to make themselves. They hid in alcoves or connecting halls, clearing a path for her. They turned to face the walls or each other, suddenly in conversation, avoiding her line of sight altogether. There was only a quiet murmur. I heard no laughter echoing these rooms, no playful squealing from children, or music.

"They are compensated for their time. They have shelter and can afford food and clothing. They are not oppressed." She looked back to me and added, "What else should they need?" I couldn't tell if she wanted a response, but I also couldn't bring myself to argue, out of fear of whatever these other people were afraid of.

As the hallways opened up again, it grew quieter. More clusters of people stood scattered, only their clothes were made of finer weaving or decorated with bones. Some didn't seem to be as intimidated as the lower classes, instead we were followed by ripples of whispered gossip. A different part of me was fascinated by the intricate carvings that stretched up towards the ceilings and distracted by the sweeping fashions of the public or the strange objects that were carried past us.

When we finally turned into a comparatively small conference room, we were nearly the only ones there. The room was still large enough to hold a meeting table for a group, and the same figure I'd blearily seen holding court before sat a little distance from the table. T'sol stood and met Neasa half-way when she strode ahead to talk with him. I couldn't distinguish their relationship at first. T'sol spoke with command but the more I observed, the more I noticed him listening closely to her response. He watched her expression as they talked quietly, before raising his voice to the rest of the people in the room. "Everybody out!"

Betraying a little of what she must have felt, Neasa's face hardened, her lips pursed. She tried to step closer, maybe attempting to say something else, but T'sol turned his back.

"My Lord," she began, only to choke. I watched from the doorway, dark shapes stalked together and drew in close. From where I stood, the cold swept over to her and I could see her hand shiver as she clawed at her throat.

"I said, everybody." He spoke in a voice just as quiet as the one he'd used when they muttered together.

The cool draft and the encroaching terror withdrew. Neasa turned abruptly and marched from the room, her forehead grave, her lips just as tense but colourless. Shortly after I felt her hand between my shoulders, pushing me forward, and the doors boomed behind me.

I was tense, I tried to stand tall though, feeling the stone beneath my feet as I took a deep breath. I was keenly aware that the shadows were still rippling around the edge of the room. I was only a moment away from returning to that place of hopelessness and cold. Of not caring.

T'sol was broader than his sisters, and his hair had been clipped short, contrary to their traditional style. I'd gotten used to seeing braids on everyone. His face was just as gaunt as those he ruled, as if he felt all of his shadow. He shared his cheekbones and jawline with his sisters.

"Woods, isn't it? I knew your father." His voice was softer than before and had lost its commanding tone.

"Yes"—I cleared my throat—"it seems many people did."

He walked to the window at the back of the room, the shadows drifted around him like oil in water, but I had to ignore them when I moved closer to hear what he was saying.

"...long shadows we have to stand in. Did they think we would be the same people when the world is so different?"

I hadn't been told if there were any formalities, but I knew there would be social rules I wasn't aware of. Recalling what I'd been told in Pelthas, I remained a few paces away from him and tried to see what the window overlooked from where I stood. It would've been my only orientation guide so far, even if I didn't recognise where to head.

"My father didn't understand that. The Unseelie were already steps ahead whilst he was busy convincing himself he'd won, blind..."

I couldn't help but wonder what the aim of our meeting was. I knew they needed my father's energy for something, I knew they had closed the gap between our worlds, which had caused the Seelie to seek refuge out of fear for this world.

"How are my sisters?" His head turned, though I couldn't read whether it was concern or scorn in his expression.

I thought of their heavy shoulders, the weight of a homeless people. "Burdened." Then, wondering if that was too honest, I added, "But they know what they need to do."

"I wouldn't expect anything less." His drawl extended to his eyes, his whites making him look just as tired as his people.

"What do you need me for?" I started after a moment of not knowing whether I should say anything else about the Seelie. "Why won't your shadow leave me alone?" That's when all this had really started, I thought with a shock, all those years ago.

Yet, why hadn't I learnt to manage it? Had the darkness accompanied me the same time as it had T'sol?

"I'm sure you understand we're dealing with timeless energies here," he said, "The problem is that time brings change, especially when you need to change something to its prior state of being." He looked at me with pity, head tilted. He waited for a response, an expression, anything that he could've read, before looking back.

"It appears that the energy you can harness is closer to that of my shade and that more primal source, than any others. From the shade's perspective, you were the quickest and easiest way to gather what it needs. You could speed all this up, but it will happen regardless, whether you're part of it or not."

Wasn't that similar to something Lunete had said? I moved slowly and tried to peer around him to the window. Past the first chimneys, the tops of buildings were a patchwork. Some were blackened from fire or half tumbled, whilst others seemed to be operating as if nothing had happened, cooking smoke joining with that coming from the streets. I might have been able to identify a gate or road if I could get closer, but the blood in my ears reminded me of the situation I'd found myself in.

"We are all part of a web. It's just the nature of our existence, but does that mean we can't decide which way to grow? If you build an empire, why shouldn't you reap what that produces? Everyone here has that opportunity." He turned again, his broad lips open in question. "So what opportunity can we offer you?"

Those who'd helped me so far hadn't had the same opportunities. I'd received food and water from down-turned eyes and blank expressions. I knew in that moment, for people to have their dreams and be provided opportunity, there were those who had to sell their very time. In some warped way, I'd just ended up back where I'd started. What alternatives were there? Was there another measure of success?

However obvious, I wasn't ready to look it in the eye. The pain of my mistakes only gave me more motivation to run.

T'sol raised both eyebrows. "Alternatively, if you don't want anything here...?"

"You'd let me go home?" I barely heard myself, so I was surprised when he responded.

He shrugged, eyes flicking back to the cityscape, "Eventually, maybe you could be courtless. It would have to go both ways; no interference with either court, and naturally that extends to either's work. In return, we won't meddle in yours. Our work will go on as planned, and the Seelie are none the wiser."

I thought of Eoghan and Oona, building their life away from all this. Hadn't that been where I'd hoped to get to? I didn't see how it would change my life in the long term, but if it meant I didn't need to find my way out from my father's shadow, I was inclined to see it as a possibility. Whether my brain was still scrambled from the lack of will I'd been put under, or I felt so disconnected from the world I'd been in before, I had forgotten all my previous wariness. I'd been left in a place where I was feeling out the rules as I went. It seemed too good to be true.

"Is that an option?"

He almost looked as if he wasn't listening, eyes rolling from one side to the other, watching outside until he turned his gaze. He slowly ground his jaw. "We all have the same time at the moment, and I'd say you're too stubborn to want anything

173

here..." He grasped my wrist suddenly. I didn't think I'd been that close when the numbness began to disperse around his fingers.

I tried to pull back. "What are you doing?" I felt something sharp at the base of my thumb and gasped. I looked from T'sol's hard eyes to the blood welling up on my palm, and just as the cold became unbearable, he let go.

The bead of blood had gone, leaving behind the open mark and a smear.

"I'll have the Pact drawn up. You'll be a little freer now but we cannot let you go home yet."

I didn't see him indicate or ring any hidden bells but the two who'd been stationed outside my hallway re-entered, staying close to the large panelled doors. He waved us away, and I was left feeling, once again, that I didn't know what had happened. Where I had left myself?

"W-wait—" I started as the guards pulled me from the room. "When can I leave?"

Chapter Twenty

"Eoghan, has there been anything?" The woman with bright hair stood between the men, one with grey hair and the other dark. A white shape on four legs waited with the group.

Because of that figure, it hadn't been able to get close to what it needed, until she came to the house. As directed, it had left something of itself with her, and it was only a matter of time, the limited time these beings had.

"Nothing yet. I can only assume they plan to keep hold of her until they feel more confident in their position." The grey man directed his sound to both other figures. "Oona has been away longer still and hasn't brought back any other news. What of the council?"

"Still takes just as long to decide anything," the woman responded. The dark-haired male began walking towards the white figure. He didn't face it directly but made himself known and waited. "They still haven't established that she didn't leave on her own, though I'm reasonably sure both sisters are in favour."

"You might have more success pushing the shared agenda: it will get the Seelie back home sooner, and they will save more of their people."

The younger male stood from touching the smaller, white one and turned back. "What are you going to do? Eoghan, I fear for her, but we can only do so much here. I fear she is easily drawn into darkness—" His voice dropped. "Could you not talk with the prime sisters?"

"As Lunete's old tutor, I will request a meeting and hope the severity of all this moves her to act with me. There was something I was hoping to do with Morgan, when she was ready, but I fear we might have to take the risk without her."

The one with dark hair relaxed his shoulders, but the woman looked between them. "Oh, please be careful, Eoghan." She gave the other one another look and said, "I don't know what we'd do without you."

Chapter
Twenty-One

Whether the Unseelie found a kind of comfort in our Pact or T'sol had consciously kept me from falling into darkness again, I was less clouded. In the times I tried to push myself into the hallways, I couldn't decide if it made my time there worse or not. In its place, at the forefront of my mind, there was a clearer realisation of where all the blame lay.

I'd left Pelthas, I'd inadvertently tried an energy that I still had no idea how to use, and then I'd selfishly bargained away any advantage the Seelie gained from my being here. All that didn't even acknowledge that I might not be able to leave either.

I busied myself with exploration again. I had already tried going further than before and hadn't been stopped again. I supposed they must have known that I was no longer able to disrupt their plans. I couldn't help but wonder what happened when the Pacts were broken though.

From what I could make out, unlike the Seelie's bartering system, value in the Unseelie market came from a subjective scale that reflected a select few. Even their everyday objects were extravagant, like plates and cutlery, and weapons that were often open and visible. I realised the decoration depended on their race, bones and stones, pelts, hair. But they all liked them to be on display.

I hadn't found my way out yet. Once, at my most determined, I'd gotten completely lost and the stretches of rooms got emptier and emptier, but I was led back by a guard who obviously wanted to be doing anything else. The following time I found myself waking up in my room, unsure whether I'd been attacked or if I'd even left at all.

Something I'd been told from stories was the risk of eating and drinking in other worlds. I had no basis to think that this was true, even when it was at the front of my mind, but eventually I had no choice. Would it bind me further to this place? Was my being here the same with my human blood? I was often woken by the smell of stew. It was similar to the stew we ate at Pelthas, and eventually I had to ease the gnawing of my stomach with small amounts of the strangely yellow bread.

Those who checked in on me were quiet. They shook their heads when I asked questions, so I started to listen to others in the hallways to see if there was another language circulating. Some answered minimally, saying it was okay or tiredness, whilst others only passed messages along to me after I'd been exploring. Neasa had apparently expected to see me once and other gatekeepers were mentioned as if their names should mean something to me.

I eventually worked out my direction, I'd systematically taken each corridor, and one day turned into the vast reception room that I'd first been taken to. The walls I hadn't made out before revealed similar carvings and reliefs to the Pelthas' entrance, histories and stories winding together into their own pattern. One wall looked charred, where ash further emphasised a past queen's features. The large object I'd glimpsed became a chair, which stood towards the rear three-quarters and behind a long, low table.

It still wasn't empty, but I wasn't noticed where I stood and watched. The rest of the space was occupied with echoing taunts, jeers, and tussles. As I passed the imposing entrance, I saw more than one armbanded hurry around with downcast eyes. It wasn't a place that I could see the less fortunate gather because of this.

Reluctant to stop when I'd got that far, it wasn't long before I found my way out to an equally large, busy courtyard. Rough stone walls rose around it in a huge arc, only to open up to the city streets I'd passed on my way in. It spanned against the horizon, immeasurable in the same way their prime house had felt so far.

Numerous streets led into the courtyard, though only one or two was clear of rubble, beggars, or smoke. A few individuals pushed basic carts, escorted by similarly dressed guards to those inside. People huddled in the crevices and watched anyone who passed, only to quickly busy themselves if they'd been caught looking. An occasional cry cut through the city sounds, making some people pause for a heartbeat, as if it were still jarring, as if they were working out whether to run. Everyone was listening and waiting.

Regardless, taking a breath outside in that moment, the air felt lighter than it was inside. I recalled Lunete talking about what I was able to pick up through the cavern walls. It was the hum I'd recognised coming from a gate source.

I was pushed aside on the stairs and, even at the carved balustrade, hesitated to drop my focus on what was happening around me. I thought that *some*thing, some area of use, must have been nearby but knew my memories couldn't be trusted. They could've carried me for miles when I'd lost consciousness. The clearer perception of my situation and my unclouded recognition left me feeling bolder than I had in the days or weeks I'd been there, so I stayed. The caves were quieter in comparison and there had obviously been walls for me to feel along. I watched people come and go, a stretch of busyness passing, and in that time, I gained my babysitters again. They watched me from the same distance and didn't move to take me back.

Gradually, the brightest part of the day disappeared and the only thing I knew for certain was that I would be taken back. But only when the foot falls, cart rattles, and general street noise began to fall to the back of my mind, could I even try to pick up anything like I'd hoped to hear.

Chapter
Twenty-Two

The grey-haired male arrived first. This one didn't move in the same group as the others, but the white one on four legs was never far away. As bidden, it followed, splitting its awareness to keep syphoning the energy it needed but also to keep watch on these camps. As usual, they clustered at the periphery of the shade's vision.

The male was soon joined by the female with long white hair and another female who it hadn't been aware of before. Shortly behind them came another two figures that were dressed like their fighters.

"Thank you for agreeing to meet me," the old one said. "It is my understanding that you're as concerned for our young gatekeeper as her friends. In front of your guards, prime sister, this ritual is not without risk. There may have been a need for me to do this with Miss Woods, but well... I'm sure you understand my position."

The white-haired one gestured in a direction and they all slowly began to move whilst she responded. "I know we've had little opportunity to speak privately since your return, but I like to believe we could have been great friends in another life. From an older perspective, I can obviously see the impact my premonition has had on your life, as well as our people, but isn't that a terrible weight for a child? Please do not think

I'm finding excuses, Master Wilkins, I am sorry, I just also feel that it's an important context if we are to attempt what you're planning."

They paused, the other female walked with the fighters behind them, when the male turned to face the white-eyed one.

"My dear, I have not held a grudge if that's what you fear. It took me a long time to get to where I am, but I do understand the obscure nature of visions. You turned to your father when it was something that scared you, like a daughter should if they need to. In a way, we wouldn't be in the same situation if I hadn't been exiled. I wouldn't have spent my life with my wife June, and you would not be the seer you are today."

The other one nodded, and her mouth turned up. "On that understanding, my guards have witnessed me saying that I came here of my own volition and that Master Wilkins is acting in our mutual interest to ensure the safety of Miss Woods." She looked over to the small group who nodded in response.

After a moment, she continued. "Master Wilkins, you requested I bring along a trusted gatekeeper. I'd like to introduce Hazel Woods. They have only recently found each other, but I can imagine no other working in her interest."

The grey one lowered his head momentarily before he said, "A pleasure. It's a comfort knowing Morgan had family nearby during her time here."

The other female joined the two that talked, walking the space in between. "The pleasure is mine. Your work in the equilibriums is foundational. Though I'm ashamed to say I probably wasn't as supportive to Morgan as I should have been; my gate has been under threat, and I haven't been here as much as I would've liked."

"We don't believe it was anyone's fault, and it is difficult to pull someone back who's already started down that road. Now"—he looked between the two—"have either of you been involved with anything like this before?"

The short-haired female shook her head whilst the other indicated to the urns and dish carried behind them. "I have scried in waters, even gate waters, but never with a keeper. I presume we are looking into Unseelie lands because there is no other way to confirm her whereabouts?"

The old one nodded and made the same gesture the white-haired one had made before. In the same manner, they continued through the trees and ferns, following the male. When they stopped again, they weren't far from the place it had been told to attack the other female traveller, the one that had hurt it. Power flowed through the river but never enough to consume, never enough to use, until she had arrived.

It watched whilst the group made a little clearing in the elbow of the waters and settled. The old one directed them, the others pausing before each filled one of the clay decanters they had carried with them. He waited for the others to sit before he filled his own and set the metal dish in the middle of their circle.

"You're welcome to stay," he called to the outside two, "but please avoid disturbing us at all costs. I cannot state enough how dangerous it will be if you do." He looked between the two another moment, before awkwardly lowering himself to the ground, legs wooden in front of him.

"Hazel, I would like you to activate these waters as you normally would a gate. It doesn't have to open. Lunete, likewise, your vision will hold us in a liminal space, and I want you both to follow my chant. In Albios, we'll be able to direct our sight to nearby areas as I might've done with Morgan. Only this time, perhaps we can gain a little more insight into what is happening."

Together, they raised the urns and poured the water into the dish. It filled quickly, but watching the old man, they all continued until the jugs were empty. It soaked into their worn fabrics as much as it spread into the earth. The grey one then started a low, echoing hum and raised his hand above the brimming dish. Resonant and in key, the females joined in. It was thrown back but immediately drawn back in, the air succulent. It watched as the three lowered their hands into the dish, the lowering notes emanating through it.

• • • •

It was a slow awareness of a different hum in the air.

As it grew louder, I grew more certain that it was the same as that in the caverns. The other sounds drowned away as I tried to concentrate on it, aware of the shifting light and streets that signified the time I'd be pulled away.

Moving again, I tried to look sure of my direction, confident, as if I was following orders when I was really trying to hear which direction I needed to go. I only doubled back twice, and the first of those, my guards hadn't caught up anyway. I grew more certain, the direction I needed to head becoming as clear as the humming ringing beneath everything else. As I went between groups of hurrying workers, herded animals and families, part of me hoped it might be enough to lose my sitters. I wasn't being led far from the prime house, the streets winding around the courtyard, next to public gardens.

I wanted to be able to find wherever this would lead. I wouldn't get the chance again if I found myself waking back in my room. Focusing on the noise's direction kept me moving, I tried not to look around. I would waste time trying to recognise anyone among the faces.

I arrived at an area that was paved in the same style as the prime house, the contrast lay in how few people there were around me. A wild looking guard leant against a nearby tree, eyes falling on the sparse public. I could see light in what I realised were nearby guardhouses. Walking in the same direction as the others, I took in the extravagantly carved gate and surrounding wall as I passed. Braided carvings spanned ahead on my left side, and there was an unmistakable trickle of water. My heart thudded in relief at the possibility of actually finding something. I followed the wall around in the same way the streets wrapped around the house. I knew I wouldn't be so lucky as to find a back entrance, but the reality was, I didn't know what to do next.

It was only when I looked around that I noticed the crowd had become airier, bigger spaces were left between each other. Because of this, I realised that the entire road I walked on was in shadow. The sun, though it was making its way down, hadn't completely dipped behind the buildings either. I'd been concentrating so much on following this lead through, that I hadn't stopped to notice the unnatural chill taking hold of the air.

It hadn't gripped me yet. I stood tense, my breath unable to sate the weight keeping me from running. Something clutched my insides and the fear of being painfully aware in the darkness began to rear up. I still didn't have anything to show. The weight pulling at my limbs might have shifted if I tried to run, but the calmness of the public made me think I was the only one aware of its presence. Either that or it wasn't anything different to them.

I couldn't see anyone else who may have been charged with watching me and, aware that trouble was only a twitch away, I was struck by the irony of looking for them now.

At that point, I decided the risk of my being attacked couldn't get any higher and thought I could use the risk for something useful. Relishing my last still second, I set my eyes behind the guardhouse before slowly heading back the way I'd come. Perhaps it was my awareness, but it writhed, agitated.

I had to bolt, I lurched, aiming for anything vaguely gate shaped. Trying to keep my mind clear, I blocked the possibility that all this had nothing to do with the gates. Even if there was a very valid possibility.

I heard a yell by the time I passed the outhouse. Outlines of trees and something particularly square formed ahead, when I suddenly couldn't remember what I had been about to do. Slowing, my limbs were struck with such a bone-weary tiredness, I was relieved at the chance to simply pause.

From where I stood, I couldn't work out if the very pressure that pinned me was numbness, a lack of feeling about anything that could've happened to me, or hopelessness. I held back a cry, resorting to silence. The squarish outline that sat a little way from the tree horizon was quickly hidden, and blackness thickened around me until it had been completely obscured. I could still make out the walls reaching around us, and it was enough for me to remember the caverns.

In vain, I reached out through the darkness, the effort finally forcing me to my knees, like my very bones ached for. Laughter from the guards walking up behind me brought my concentration back for the second time, but whatever they said next was clouded by humming. It was different to the sound I'd followed here, three or four voices harmonised in a tune I hadn't heard before. I held on to it, a lifeline in the suffocating black. It wasn't that I trusted it, but I followed it wherever it took me because there was nothing else.

I couldn't have said when I went from reality to dream. My awareness rose in a situation I couldn't be sure wasn't real. Eoghan, Lunete, and Hazel, whom I'd only met a few times, were all walking into the very courtyard I'd just left. At first, I followed, confused. I recognised all of these elements, but, like in a dream, I didn't understand what was wrong. Had I finally been rescued? Had the Seelie won the last battle?

The three of them looked around at the courtyard. It must have been very different in its previous life but it was in the same state of neglect as I'd left. Sadness broke out on all their faces in different ways: in Eoghan's frown and forehead, in Lunete's posture, Hazel's stillness.

"It might be worth talking to the people," I said behind them, thinking about their haunted expressions. No one looked my way, and I didn't connect this in my daze until they moved inside, the same guards in rotation. All at once, it was one oddity too many, and I could feel my lucidity return, it was Eoghan murmuring to the others.

"I know we won't have time to search the whole house, but if Morgan's here, our focus on her should help. It would be prudent to not act rashly. We cannot know how much awareness the shadow has, even in spaces like these."

"Eoghan," I said, about to rest a hand on his arm when they continued to move.

Only Lunete paused, her eyes resting on me long enough to think it was real, before she headed in the direction of the big entrance hall with the others. My breath went with them, and I couldn't help but wonder if I'd stranded myself in an even worse situation.

I knew I had run. I recognised that we must have been on the same day or else this was all in my head. The same guards were on duty, the same heckling groups patrolled their chosen spots, the same immobile beggars with their recent collection of beatings. The question more concrete than my grasp on reality was whether they were actually there. If it was my subconscious manifesting itself, I should have admitted how little I'd tried to myself.

I continued to follow them, and we walked through a few spaces I was familiar with, each step seeming to cover three to five paces, hallways blurring. More than once, Lunete watched a family go about their given duty, a child tugging at their guardian for food they obviously didn't have. Hazel let out a gasp when brawling henchmen were pushed out of one wide hallway into our path.

I had to trust that they knew where they were heading, but their hesitancy and care revealed how dangerous this really was. Soon, I began to realise they headed towards the room I'd met T'sol in, though I couldn't do anything about my growing apprehension. During my time there, I'd assumed the conference room was where he dealt with more everyday business. The thriving fear of the shadow chimed somewhere between my heart and throat.

"Eoghan, Lunete," I called, somehow registering their risk would be higher there, but neither turned. Taking some fast steps to get ahead of Hazel, I tried reaching again, only for her to inadvertently step around me. Eoghan entered the room, and I could only watch as they all registered who they'd found. Eoghan immediately turned and used his arm to indicate they should leave again.

Lunete continued to walk forward, her expression fixed on hearing the reports each figure voiced. T'sol sat at the head of the table, the same spot where I'd broken the only rule I'd been given. Neasa sat to his right, and I recognised about half the other henchmen from the halls. I stood just as still as the others, barely breathing, for fear of breaking the spell that kept us unseen.

"...tribes of púca are still working on the western areas, where they've had previous success. The more resources we're able to gather—"

"There is enough!" The largest figure there slammed their great claw down. "We need to destroy the gates for the rest of the chronoscopic power we need. How much longer will our good fortune—"

"Watch your tongue!" Neasa snapped, her eyes locked the figure in place. "I have not spent my life in pursuit of my father's revenge for scum like you to call it divine..."

Lunete had drawn even closer to her brother, her brow furrowed as if reliving their childhood growing up and their parents' deaths all at once.

"T'sol... in those years in between, I hoped and hoped my prophesy wasn't about you..."

Her brother raised his hand suddenly, pausing the argument that had broken out. Eoghan stepped forward, obviously sharing the adrenaline the simple gesture had caused.

"My Lord?" The figure said, echoing the expectation at the table. T'sol tilted his head, listening. Neasa watched with open fascination.

He stood suddenly and, before any of us could reach Lunete, reached past the veil and gripped her throat. He'd made piercing it look so easy.

"No!"

"Lunete!"

"T'sol..." She was just as surprised as everyone else, eyes wide and hands on her brother's wrist. "H-how?..."

Eoghan didn't move. He closed his eyes, murmuring something under his breath. How could you defend yourself when you weren't really there? Knowing I might be to either side's advantage, I leapt in for him. I darted around the chairs that had been pushed out in surprise and reached for Lunete. But I couldn't reach her. The closer I thought I got, the further away I became.

"I can't move my hand from the water! There must be something else interfering!" Hazel looked wildly between her partners, shivering, face dampened with sweat. Eoghan swiftly raised his hands and sucked in. For a minute, the shadows were drawn his way, slinking into a vortex and contorting T'sol's expression. But, resolute, it sped back the next minute quicker than before.

"My Lord, what is it?" T'sol's council was still curious, and I lost track of how many layers of sight there were. I joined Eoghan and Hazel where they stood, where Lunete wasn't quite with them but also couldn't quite have been in Albios. As if confirming my suspicions, T'sol looked at me like Lunete had before and then turned back to his table. The sinking sickness in my stomach told me I hadn't been able to help because of our deal. No interfering.

"My loyal friends, I'd like to introduce my youngest sister," T'sol said in a malicious tone as he pulled Lunete through. She stumbled and must have landed in Albios as the Unseelie Council at the table stood in uproar, shouting.

Neasa's eyes lit up and she clapped excitedly. "A present! A spy... did she come alone?"

Though T'sol had let go of Lunete now, I couldn't stop watching her. Eoghan and Hazel backed out, obviously torn between not abandoning a council member and fear for their own safety. They couldn't help anyone if they got caught too.

Like before, I didn't know when I realised it wasn't a dream. Even if it had just been from Eoghan's pushing, and Áine and Drust's encouragement, I hoped their visit meant the Seelie had done something. As much as that reassurance warmed my heart, it made my chest burn at the risk they'd taken too. It had been a risk for me, and now they didn't have their seer.

Hazel was reluctant to leave, maybe holding to see what they might do, but Eoghan pulled her away. T'sol's head inclined like before, listening again, as his council passed comments and jokes about Lunete. She too looked like she was concentrating, perhaps trying to grasp whatever had allowed them to travel here. Quietly, under the ruckus coming from the table, I heard her hum. It was like the tune I'd heard before all this. I reached out, trying again, but she was jostled.

Intermittently, from his concentration, T'sol began shaking his head as if something irritated him. Out of his table, only Neasa noticed, her eye catching without saying anything. As my memories pieced themselves together, I didn't think I would really be able to get in trouble for being there. The shadow was aware of where I was and therefore T'sol probably was too, and, as agreed, I hadn't been able to interfere with the actions of the Seelie. If anything, it could've been some kind of spectacle. Would they threaten Lunete to force me to help them? How would she want me to act?

As if the shadow were spread too thin, it had lost its opacity and the very air swirled with it. Natural shadows of the furniture and walls smoked, giving the air texture.

"Enough," T'sol said to those around him, but some kind of argument had broken out and only those who'd been watching him noticed. Moving as quickly as her skirts allowed, Lunete darted around me, perhaps sensing the hysteria that was to follow, but Neasa was quicker. She gripped her arm, holding her back from leaving.

His voice suddenly rose above all other noise. "Out! Now!" Then, resuming at his normal volume, added, "I would like to talk to my sister."

Whilst there was movement to the door, Neasa's stony gaze said that she thought that was a particularly bad idea. She waited until everyone else had left, and I wondered how long I had left in this space. I knew it could be my only opportunity to hear some of this. If I listened carefully, my mind still buzzed with Eoghan and Hazel's hummed incantation. Had they made it back safely?

"My Lord, are you sure you shouldn't rest first?" Neasa said woodenly, nails digging into Lunete's dark skin more than T'sol's had. I recognised her look as 'this is something we should talk about'. The anger I'd expected to see didn't rear again. Instead, T'sol sunk heavily into his chair, slouching and putting his feet up on her chair. He continued to look at her expectantly.

Neasa's eyes narrowed, but she thrust Lunete back towards him before standing by the door, out of earshot. As soon as she turned, T'sol's head dropped into his hand, evidently drained from using the shadow in such a way.

"Our mother would not rest if she saw you now," Lunete said, arms wrapped around herself. I tentatively moved closer to hear what was being said.

Without opening his eyes, T'sol didn't wait before responding. "Our mother all but disowned me with the others after your damned prophecy."

"Oh T'sol, can't you see by now that you fulfilled it yourself?" She paused before asking, "Who was it? Who was your Unseelie tutor?"

From a face that I had only ever seen under control, it was a surprise when he started snickering, his eyes wide but untouched by his laughter. Concern etched itself in Lunete's forehead and I wondered if his health had been part of his price. When he finally looked up, he nodded his head towards Neasa. Her hard stare falling on them alternately.

There was silence and for a moment, it jarred me. Until Lunete spoke, I hadn't realised I had still been listening to their humming. But without it, I noticed that Eoghan's baritone and Hazel's harmony had finally stopped.

"Your orphan friend," she whispered, after placing Neasa's dark hair and pointed face. "But who?" Everything was still.

"Understand, I am doing what's best for us all." His voice broke, though he quickly continued. "Our house wouldn't have survived another war, and as rightful leader, it's my duty..."

I could still see that T'sol was talking but the stillness around me grew. White noise filled my ears, and I could feel something pulling at my consciousness. I held on, curious about what I'd learn and filled with the need to watch over Lunete. But, as if I'd been injected with something, the next thing I knew, I was waking up in my room again.

Chapter
Twenty-Three

I had no way of confirming that what I'd seen was real. No word of Lunete's arrival reached me, and my prison remained the same. I hoped they simply thought I'd been trying to escape. If T'sol had seen me like my gut told me, surely it would be only a matter of time before Lunete was threatened.

I begged the armbanded to speak to me, to help me. I could get them out, I promised, desperate enough to risk not knowing for certain. My daze returned sevenfold, and the guards at the end of the hall remained, their eyes hollow, their antlers molting and bloody. I tried to keep my behaviour the same, but the thought of leaving needed more energy than my limbs had. Eventually, I assumed it was leftover from the attack and, without meaning to, another week passed around me.

After a while, one of the women who brought me food must have felt sorry for me. She looked about my age. Sitting me up, she helped me wash and gently combed out my hair. My thoughts moved through tar, but the quiet understanding between us felt enough. She started leaving me little trinkets with my morning fruit. An iridescent shell, a long bunch of grass flowers in multiple hues of red, a small drawing of a masculine face, their strange curving letters wrapped around it like a blessing.

Without the will or strength to do anything else, the mere fact that she found that little bit more in herself for me made my eyes hot and my throat tighter than it already was. With something more to think about, I saw her gifts as what they were— the things she was freely giving because she could. It made me think of Áine and her sisters, holding on to each other because it didn't matter what else they had or didn't have. I thought of Urien losing his son, grieved by the whole community, and holding each other up. I thought about everyone having a say in what they did, and I couldn't understand why it hadn't been enough for me. It fit who I imagined my family to be and could see the happy life we might have led if there hadn't been war. I thought of Olivia, my one close friend back home who helped me paddle, and Joanne, who had done the same for Mum.

If my father had known the next battle was on the horizon, if he was aware of what the Unseelie were planning, protecting his seemingly human family would have been his first priority. Wanting to hold his key and draw comfort from an imagined closeness, I began to search my pockets. When I couldn't find it, I moved to my coat, fitful, but it was gone. It hadn't been something I thought they'd take. It wasn't important. But its loss felt too much to bear in that moment when I didn't have anything else.

The days blurred into one, which meant it was one long night thinking about what I should've done and all the things I couldn't do now. Only the woman's little gifts seemed to break up the monotony. Sometimes she would clear them away, as if they were merely things I'd dragged in on my clothes. But just like the objects in Mum's shop so long ago, I couldn't help but imagine what that stone or piece of carving had seen. How had it come to be and who had it known?

Sometimes I would ask her if I could keep something, and only once did she look over the few trinkets I'd kept already. My prized piece was a small animal skull, a reminder of the time I'd spent and wasted that I wouldn't see again. I tried to hold on to the idea that I really didn't know how long it had been, and the jab of panic it brought helped me manage.

I knew I wanted to find Lunete if she was still alive. I knew I owed it to Olivia and Joanne to try to get back home. I knew that if I finally lost myself in a way of life, anything I wanted to fill it with would be better than living like this. I wanted to be able to give in return. I knew I might need to find the Pact archives I'd heard so much about.

Beginning small, I neatly tore a large leaf she'd given me into a rough square. Probably only a day or two old, it wasn't yet crispy but the folds I made creased enough to hold. With just one mistake, I presented a basic flower to my friend the next time I saw her. The warmth I felt from her smile told me that she felt the same when she did it for me. She tucked it away carefully. I wonder now if she also knew that it meant a revival of some kind. It was all out of my reach. I couldn't change anything around me and only by seeing what else there was, could things change, could things be influenced again. I could only change what I did.

As she left, the lock didn't fully catch. It had not been locked before, I'd already checked that, but somehow the lure of the outside sneaking in through that window was all I needed to get up again.

. . . .

Neasa tracked me down on one of these excursions. I had found a balcony that was nearly always empty, the common route leading away as it overlooked one of the busier areas. Sitting side-on to the hall but watching those below, I noticed her figure come towards me. I knew what to expect now and kept my eyes following what I could see of the shadow. Was this to get me involved again? Were they about to tell me about Lunete?

It had kept me on edge being here. I was now awake enough to know the darkness was everywhere, and knew I'd have to keep myself steady to avoid drawing its attention or I risked a deeper drop the more I got involved. The time spent in my head allowed me to observe its changes.

"You didn't look like the type to succumb so quickly," Neasa said half under her breath, examining my blank features. "Maybe it wouldn't be such a loss to force your hand."

My eyes fell on her, and I hoped to show my lack of amusement. I hoped my silly deal stopped them from forcing my hand too. A corner of her mouth tilted, cruel pleasure in the planes of her face.

"What did T'sol promise you?"

I continued to watch her for a second, attempting to control my face as I realised he hadn't told her. Which meant that those Pact archives weren't an option. How guarded were they if Neasa couldn't access them? And how little could I say? Though it felt like she oversaw much of what went on here in the city, it also felt like T'sol held the upper hand due to his control of the shadow.

"I don't think he made any promises." It wasn't a lie. "I just didn't want to be involved with any of this." As nonchalantly as I could, I turned back to the dull-eyed public, who hurried from one hallway to the next or sat as quietly as I was in corners and along the walls. There didn't seem to be much in between. I tried to take on the same careless look, disdain for everything that kept me here. Neasa lifted a hand and grazed a long nail along my temple. It was powdered in black, the same way I'd noticed others in court wearing their nails. She tucked a stray lock of hair behind my ear.

"And what do you want now?"

"Nothing," I replied after a moment of imagining what everyone else would say. "I'm just trying to survive."

She lifted an eyebrow, and I couldn't be sure if she believed me. "Is that what you were trying to do when you left the house and went into Falias?"

I hadn't been that far again yet and wondered if it hadn't been that long, "I was only trying to stretch my legs. Sometimes I wake up and think I haven't been out at all." I added, watching her in my periphery. I couldn't know what information made its way back to her, so I had to assume all.

Whilst her stare burrowed into the side of my face, perhaps working out if I knew anything else, she seemed somewhat satisfied. She stood to leave, and I couldn't stop myself thinking that if they wanted me to remain lifeless and unthinking, herding my thoughts and finding a way to do anything at all was my best resistance.

My sitters remained in sight, even as she took her leave. I released a satisfying breath but remained where I was, watching through the carved balustrade. Neasa didn't walk back through my sight and so must have headed towards the more maintained rooms.

I had long assumed the shadow clouded my consciousness and had seen its effects in others too, but something lingered at the back of my mind, nudged by Neasa's visit. When I'd woken up from my vision of Eoghan and Hazel, I'd tried to go over the details, in case there'd been something important. The fact that T'sol and Neasa had been friends—or at least accomplices—for a long time had escaped me. Though T'sol had been the one to take the lives that created the living darkness, had she planned it? She had been around the prime family for a long time, slowly manipulating the situation and T'sol's life, but to what end?

The longer I sat there, I felt like I was seeing how things unravelled. Watching the people below being preyed upon, I was simultaneously reminded that the Unseelie Council had talked about time, and that Eoghan, a lifetime ago at my first meeting, had theorised the dark creature may have been collecting something.

I thought of how my days had slipped into one since I'd been here. I thought of the unquenchable pit that weighed me down since we'd left my father's house. I thought of the childhood fear that had followed me, the dark side of life, hiding where you least expected it, out of sight. The longer I thought about it, the more it made sense. Was that what the shadow was collecting? Didn't the very gates that my father's family protected traverse the time gap between our worlds? Hadn't even that disappeared when T'sol had created the darkness?

It was only a matter of waiting, T'sol had said. It was only a matter of time.

I knew Eoghan was clever enough to piece this together as well. I knew that Drust had probably already learnt so much more about the shadow's nature. Some part of me hated how much I felt like I owed them. All of their patience and care when I hadn't realised I'd needed it yet, how much they all had going on in their own lives. I had been selfish in a nation of selfless people. I had been so focused on what I'd needed at the time, I hadn't stepped back to see that it required less effort to help everybody as they helped me, rather than more on my own.

I realised this too late of course, helping the Seelie was now as out of reach as helping the Unseelie. Unless I could find a way to change our Pact. In all my watching, I hadn't seen anything that resembled paper, so wherever they were sealing these documents, they didn't go far. As I headed back that night, I resolved to find out if the vision had been real. I needed to help Lunete if I could. I needed to reach the limit of what I could do against our deal. And hope it was enough to show me the next step.

Chapter
Twenty-Four

When I next left my room, I was able to walk around more like I used to and my regular sitters weren't in sight. Still uncertain of the layout, I tried to head in the direction I thought prisoners might be kept. It probably wasn't far from where I was. I followed the more obnoxious races, and eventually cries similar to those outside rose throughout the halls. It wasn't any less busy, but I made a conscious effort to avoid anyone's attention and act as small as possible. The reality was that I wouldn't be saved if I got caught up in one of these groups. They seemed like they were their own nations.

The further I walked, the worse the conditions grew. I passed halls of workers standing at tables, each charged with making an extravagant piece of clothing, fingers bloodied. I passed groups of henchmen lining people up, intimidating them by force if they turned away, spraying the walls with blood and spit. I saw crowds outside equally unkempt infirmaries, crying or clutching, underfed children. Adolescents shadowed the guards, forming the beginnings of their own gangs.

When I casually tried to enter the more heavily guarded areas, someone with carved tusks caught my arm and pushed me back to the halls I was allowed to be in. I didn't want to waste another indefinable amount of time and pushed myself to continue. I didn't think I'd be able to search for Lunete in that hall again anyway, but I could wait for the change of the guards. And I hadn't yet exhausted trying to find where the scribes worked. I couldn't recall Áine or anyone else on the council saying it had been destroyed.

After I found my way back to the vast corridors that acted like crossroads, I waited at the side. Those in red armbands carried wide trays, weaving between others struggling under vats of water. Though I hadn't seen anything that looked like paper or writing instruments, I simply hoped to get a sense of where other labourers were working. I was jostled a few times and warned about being a disturbance by a figure that looked as if they hadn't worked a day in their life. It made the surrounding disparity even clearer, they outright ignored those who weren't able to work.

Following people who were impassive and unadorned, it wasn't long before I found the passages further back in the prime house. Immense, slanted, gaps towards the ceiling looked over the canal that cut off the rest of the city. The panes were jagged, and I wouldn't have been surprised if they'd once been filled with glass. Crates were piled up along the pathway, some torn open and battered, others were guarded by different labourers who would shake their heads at those passing. I was aware that the rooms I sought might be patrolled, even so I carefully peered into the open places as I went by.

In one, the sinewy guards I now associated with the Unseelie were hunched over a carved table, the outline looked like some kind of raised map. I slowed, they were arguing but talking too fast for me to fully understand. I caught snippets about farms and supply lines. In another room, people in both plain, and finer clothes were striding between abacus-like systems. Some made notes when they'd obviously come to a decision. None of these were truly supervised like my last search, though it felt more appropriate, and I was sure I had found the more bureaucratic district.

Hoping the Unseelie didn't place as much importance on the Pacts as the Seelie did, I pushed on. The thought that these huge archives, stacked like a grand library, were probably sealed and vaulted played at the back of my mind. I eyed another mezzanine after bobbing on my heels to see how far the open corridor spanned. It grew quieter further on, but I had found that quieter often meant more security, and the more cautious I was, the more attention I attracted.

Opting to find the hidden access to the level above, I had learnt that these corridors followed a pattern. There were false walls obscuring the way in, even though many were still decorated which made finding them complicated. The public staircases led to two levels of street-like hallways and were wider and more easily accessible. Like the odd section that looked as if it'd been built later, the vast spaces nearly always contained these extra half floors, some ran all the way around, some were accessed by different stairs. It hadn't taken me long to realise that I could spend most of my life looking for new areas.

When the third flight of stairs led me into a darkened hallway, I nearly turned to come back another day. A darkened hallway could mean a whole extra passage of passages. The routes that wound further in often didn't seem logical, and at first, I felt like this was going to end like the others— with me groping along a wall, blood pounding in my ears, in the pitch black. As I made my way back from the second passage, mention of the Seelie made me pause.

Three figures stood at the top of the winding staircase, blocking my way out. "I heard it from Bran, they know of a traveller. They said the Seelie are finally preparing for battle again—"

"Too risky to act unless we're absolutely certain. We've lost enough—"

"I would rather die than find a way to live here. I'm exhausted."

"The next sign we get will make it certain..."

I had to wait for them to disperse, but I thought the possibility of the Seelie's counterattack was worth it.

I started to head back. The hallways and stairs blurred though, where they all looked so similar, and I got disorientated. I kept my movements slow and quiet just in case, and when a distant voice reached me, I flattened myself against the side, hiding my lantern. My eyes were useless when this happened, so I focused on my ears, attempting to hear where the murmurs were coming from.

It didn't get any louder and there was only one muffled voice. When my initial panic dulled, I slid my feet gently to my right, thinking about the death wish I must've had to even risk another attack. Eventually though, I grew more confident and held onto the fact that nothing had happened so far, and gradually the voice became clearer.

By the time I had to shrink down to hear it more clearly, I realised I'd come across a place to eavesdrop. It sounded very much like the prime son, though I couldn't be sure when I could only make out, "about...h-...books...-ay...Fath- was obsessed."

I sunk to the floor, hand following the cold grate I had come across.

"I remember the gesture Mother would give him when he got that look. I don't care if you know this because you won't see the Seelie Council again, but my mind sometimes feels broken, and I can't always remember what's real. But I do remember the obsession everyone had with being remembered. Carve my name, paint my deeds, know me, tell stories about me. You were his way into the records, his seer daughter. Stupid man, really, not learning more about how it worked. We all know how that ended. 'Papa, someone close, someone favoured, papa, I saw those unhappy people again.'..." His voice took on a high, childish imitation.

"So why didn't you talk to him?" a softer voice asked.

Lunete. I'd found her. Except I hadn't. How was I to find that room below once I made it back?

"'Papa, why doesn't T'sol look like the rest of us?'" He slowly dropped the inflection until he spoke again in his own voice. "'Papa, what's wrong with his heart?' Because I could tell you the day I stopped being his son as well, and you were the only one who really listened to me afterwards. Despite all that, I can still remember the life I was supposed to have. We can't all embrace exile and find a new life."

"You would have had a place at the council. You are still our brother."

"A mock position." His voice raised momentarily. "I wouldn't be listened to. I had already been judged. But I can make real changes in a rank like this."

"It's a council." I could hear the placation turn to disbelief in her tone. "If your views are in the minority, you might not get everything you want. We are not the exception, look at what happens."

There was a pause, and I came back to myself, trying to piece the fragments together.

"I have to do this," T'sol said. "Things will improve."

"I can see why you might think that. But you have to see that all this is the result of your decisions."

I wanted to shout down to her, send a message somehow about what I'd just heard in the hallways. Help could be on its way, but I couldn't bear to be the reason that failed as well, so I stayed still, listening as long as I could.

"I want to be able to forgive you, T'sol. I want to have the brother back who looked after me, who made light over breakfast, I miss when our family was whole."

I heard a deep murmur, where T'sol must have responded too quietly to hear.

"It's not too late if you actually mean it..."

Chapter
Twenty-Five

Though it barely felt like I'd mapped how things worked, I could pick out the changes in those around me as soon as they started happening. People were more frantic, more reckless, shouting in the corridors, and more likely to ignore the patrols. In a way, they had resembled the Seelie again. They were worried about their loved ones and knew everything might change again. This was still home for many.

When I was able to leave the prime house again, it confirmed that my sitters were gone and likely called away to the larger numbers of uniformed patrols. Seeing them together made me realise the force the Unseelie had behind their public threats, the seemingly innocent appearance until a threat was on the horizon. As I wandered, there were more groups like those I'd seen in the backways, conspiratorial and whispering. A group not too far from the shallow stairs talked about the Seelie, openly deciding whether to join them or whether it was all a trick. They weren't as careful as the others I'd seen.

The public didn't seem to realise that was one of their collective changes either— their willingness to begin finding each other to talk to and conspire for something better. There was a sudden shared feeling of resilience. I heard an attendant preach in a dining space that the shadow had been weakened, and I felt awake enough to know it could've been true. I realised how much I still relied on others, and it was only when I could see past that smoky weight that I wanted to help those emerging from their own stupor. I still saw my friend every now and then, but I could tell her priorities had shifted. Everyone was distracted.

On a particularly restless day, the hive mind was on the verge of revolt, and there was clearly a direction the people in the hallways were heading. I hadn't found the archives yet, and I hadn't found a way to help Lunete either, but whatever was happening was enough for people to overlook their safety. When I followed, henchmen lined the way into the meeting room I'd initially seen T'sol in. They used force if anyone acted threateningly or didn't follow their direction. The flow of the crowd divided between trying to leave the prime house, heading deeper in, or into the vast chamber. Like fish, if a fight broke out, they continued around. More than ever, I felt as if I was part of the shoal.

I moved into the open space, quickly hiding my face when I spotted T'sol in the middle. Behind Neasa and the faces I'd seen at the council table, he was surrounded by an arc of a wide, tall race. It had felt like everyone was heading there, but the space wasn't filled, and I wondered if it showed any kind of loyalty. There had to be others that were curious like me too.

The doors remained open when one of the council members began shouting, "...and I can confirm that there have been attacks. They do not recognise the authority with which we reside in power. However, through the great effort of our son T'sol, a mole has been found."

Between shoulders, I saw the council member gesture towards an antechamber I hadn't noticed before. Two guards made their way through the crowd, pushing through and leaving a tunnel. Held on both sides, Lunete trailed behind, her long ruffled hair falling around her shoulders. There were cries of 'Lunete!' and 'Prime daughter!' all around me. Several guards shoved the crowd in an attempt to threaten them into order. I heard the smack of flesh on flesh, and someone shouted that a name I didn't recognise had tried to reach her.

Whilst another member continued shouting over the disruption, I used my less than Seelie stature to shoulder between the rows of watching spectators.

"Have the Seelie lost all their lofty morals? What happened to honour and fairness?"

By the time Lunete was held at the edge of the council circle, I watched a few rows back from the perimeter. I didn't have a plan and I knew that this was a bad idea, but I needed to know she was okay.

"Do you think the Seelie Council will trade for another generation of peace for her safe return?"

Some of the crowd began pressing back towards the guard-lined space. One shout bled into the next, and I could feel that the tension might spark at the first sign of skirmish. Like a ripple back out to safety, I could see the spaces between the crowd widen as others felt the same agitation and tried to escape. Or perhaps they were the first to see how the shadows around us were responding, gathering around our feet. I was focused on Lunete and didn't feel it until afterwards again.

"My dear sister." T'sol's voice rose above the crowd's murmur. "Before my court, I would like to know what you were doing trespassing on an Unseelie Council meeting?"

Lunete's white eyes were fixed on his direction.

"Louder, please." His comment was accented by a loud hitch of breath as if catching his toe. His detour from the expected caught some people, and the crowd hushed a fraction, curious about what had happened.

Lunete's voice rang above the rest.

"I didn't know what I'd find there, or where I was at first, it's not something—"

She was interrupted by his shout. From where I stood, I watched T'sol double over and catch himself on Neasa's arm, his eyes wide.

"Stand up!" Neasa spat quietly.

The henchmen stepped forward, eyes narrowed. Lunete was left standing alone between two more perimeter guards, and even they were a reasonable space apart. I knew I would never get the opportunity again. I found my way through easily enough, and so told myself I'd be able to find my way out just as easily. I could only hope that my ghostlike state from before had been from our shifting state, at least until Lunete was pulled through.

Before I knew what I was doing, before I gave myself time to think that the darkness would be particularly close by, I lunged forward, pushing past the remaining people, and reached for her arm.

"Morgan!" I heard her call. I got back to where I was a moment ago, and my limbs froze.

She caught up to me, then perhaps realising what had happened, said softly, "We're all just finding our own way, as you need to do. I'm sorry you've been caught up in all this—"

The henchmen that escorted Lunete immediately pulled her free of my grip and I was left alone under their scrutiny. People around us moved away, disassociating themselves, our own droplet of space was soon absorbed by the larger space I'd just tried to escape. I felt the dread pool at the back of my neck and down my spine. I had exposed my intentions. Neasa laughed behind me, murmuring to someone. She sounded pleased that she could see some aspect of our deal. Was she satisfied that I wasn't a threat? I knew I shouldn't have done it. But I would have wondered if I *could* have done something.

The hum of noise around me dropped, and after a moment or two, T'sol appeared in my periphery. Though his face was controlled, betraying nothing of the pain he'd just been in, he paced around to face me and stood notably tense. Like it had been called, the shadow collected around his hand.

"Ms Woods, this would be what happens when your Pact is breached." His voice was quieter, spiteful, and I could feel the shadow around me eager to please. "Whatever you were hoping to do would be an interference to Unseelie affairs. If you'll excuse me, I'm sure you understand that I have far more than your indecisiveness to manage."

He strode past me and raised his voice to the remaining spectators. There was scattered laughter and one of the council members took over, listing the city districts that had been commandeered for their troops. I was pushed back into the crowd, the sparse press of people barely kept me from landing on the floor. My shoulder ached where a guard had pushed me as if their malice was spreading through the pain.

213

I thought about the acquaintances I'd made in the Seelie, the guards that were stationed around Pelthas, in my same task groups, and didn't want them believing anything untrue about me. I wanted to see Áine and Olivia again, I wanted more discussions with Eoghan, and Drust. I had actively avoided seeing people back home but hadn't yet worked out why he was different, the understanding that had grown between us. I couldn't swallow the ache of regret out of my throat.

Moving further back into the public, I kept my head down as I listened to more of what was being said. The only thing I was grateful for was that the Pact had given me some measure of independence. They were either so confident in their deals or they simply didn't have the resources to keep me under constant watch. The crowd churned again when there were calls for workers. I didn't think there'd be any more information about what was happening outside the city and the press heading back towards the doors likely thought the same thing.

My intention was still to find the archives, and I was suddenly aware at how blatant that next step might seem. It was either that or waiting to be sent home, which I could no longer do. I was shoved from behind and only just caught myself. Something was pressed into my hand. By the time I looked around, I couldn't be sure which direction they might have gone. There was a shorter person a step away from my hand, who was talking with someone in an armband, whilst someone ahead of us pulled a child along after them.

I felt something scrunched up, soft edges made me think it was paper and I kept my hand closed around it until I was clear of the crowd. I found my alcove quiet, and I unravelled it.

The letters were curved, like written Sindaric, but written in English. It had been scrawled in a hurry with misspelt words, but it was easy enough to read.

'Wich cort are you with? We meet after super wer Nuadha's sord is held up.' Was this a trick? The only reason the Unseelie would sneak me a note would be as bait. The other possibility was Seelie conspirators. If they were in the prime house with me, at the very least I thought I could talk to them without causing an infraction.

· · · ·

That night, I waited until the hallway outside my room was quiet before slipping down to the lower levels. I carried the small lantern that was usually left in my room, the gear on its side as dim as it allowed. Many of the places that had been patrolled during the day now lay open, the henchmen on their route or commanded out into the city. Did they feel that their threat was close?

When I'd eaten that night, I tried to recall any mention of the referenced story. I knew Nuadha had lost his right to rule, and that his sword wielded old magic like the stone, but so many of their stories were recorded in their murals. And I just wasn't sure about which corridor that one was in.

I moved quietly and confidently when passing anyone. When it became more silent still, the last people falling into their districts, any reason I might've been out became less valid. So I started to hide instead. The passages looked different at night and scouting around in the dark hadn't been something I was eager to do before. The shadows collected in the tall ceilings and around the carvings I passed. Relief features deepened and spread when I walked by, suddenly dramatic. I had the impression that Nuadha's mural wasn't far from the administrative rooms I'd seen, possibly a level or two either way, so I knew I'd need time to try and locate it. I didn't trust many of the other people I saw throughout my day, and my friend hadn't been around, otherwise she probably would've walked with me if I'd asked.

I ducked into a staircase when I heard muttering and nearby movement, hiding my light just in time, when a set of guards headed the way I'd been. After another moment of waiting, I checked before continuing. I tried to move swiftly but fell back on myself when I nearly walked into another pair. At this point, I realised I was lost and lucky if I even made it to that meeting.

"Identify yourself," a deep voice said from around the corner.

My heart thumped, and I ran. I didn't know what to do, and turned off my lantern, holding it to my chest to stop its creaking. The sounds of movement passed, but I knew I wouldn't have long. Keeping my breath under control, I found my way in the dark, running my hand along the wall.

Like when I entered Pelthas, a whisper-quiet hum started beneath my fingers. At some point, I stopped running from the henchmen behind me and started following the energy I could feel in the rock, the urgency I felt for both outweighing each other. It made me want to stand up tall, confident, and made my scalp tingle. If this was old magic and potential time, it made me feel the moments when I could hold my own, when I'd managed what I wanted to do and everything was balanced, when I didn't look over my shoulder at the darkness that was only a day away. With the shroud lifting, I didn't know whether it was my own awareness or the shadow's weaker density that I could somehow feel.

I rested a moment, listening for any movements that would echo in the corridor. After I was certain I'd lost the guards, I turned on the lantern, casting a small ring of light around me. And I froze.

Shadows stalked and jumped at the edge of the light, snapping. Against the brink, I could see it writhing, waiting… but for what? How long had I been walking that path already?

I nearly got up from resting on the wall when the energy behind me beat in time with my blood, and suddenly I knew that my lantern had nothing to do with it. In the same way I'd realised I had been lost before, the idea I might've found something connected with the possibility of doing something good. Another gate? Would I try to leave? Could I help others leave?

Raising the light again and keeping my other hand against the hum I could feel in my core, I continued slowly for the next few minutes. It led, sloping down, and eventually opened up into another vast chamber.

Chapter
Twenty-Six

I entered through one of a few entrances, they were all scattered around the edge of the nearly empty cavern. The ceiling disappeared into the darkness that still surrounded me, a sentinel in its own right. Water trickled down the walls, carved arches and worn statues betrayed that I was in a sacred space. Symbols I couldn't make out were etched into the rock, some filled and covered with mosses, hinting at the events that had taken place here.

At the far end of the cave, the inlet of water was dark, but the surface mirrored the light I still held, casting reflections upon the overhanging arc. Underneath the archway, a seemingly ordinary light-grey chunk of stone was nestled in the water, its face looking up.

The air was cool and damp, the faint scent of earth rose to meet me. Just like Pelthas, I understood that if the public upstairs knew about this place, it would not be as well preserved, but I also knew I probably wouldn't be able to find it again.

I was reluctant to move away from the edge and spared a look back into the darkness that enveloped my way back out. Fear of waking up back in my room, another day wasted, drove me on. Moving slowly around the threshold, I realised that the shadow lingered around the dome of the cavern. Whilst its edges smoked and blinked out of existence when it tried to stalk me, I could feel it drawing on the energy emanating from the waters, redirecting it. The reverberation grew from my hand until I could feel it in my core, the deep thrum diverting into the tunnels I had just come out of.

Time seemed to stand still, leaving me with a vague sense of peace and contentment. As I tentatively stepped away from the walls, I reminded myself of the minutes that trickled by. Even though the worlds of the Seelie and Unseelie were still volatile, all I could think was how Eoghan had theorised something like this all those months ago, about how the misunderstood visions of a child had thrown an entire people into turmoil, about the families that had been broken apart.

Was this considered Unseelie business? I was the only one here and, although this was likely their arrangement, I felt it could just as easily be used by the Seelie or even any courtless being. I looked back to the perimeter the shadow lurked at, did darkness have a natural inclination?

The floor was covered in dirt. I had to step around a few fallen rocks and weeds that had somehow survived. As I walked towards the lake and the stone, there was no doubt about the cave's divinity. Whispers of long-forgotten hopes and dreams hung in the air, potential destinies, potential worlds to travel. I knew Eoghan, and maybe even Drust, would have ideas on how to restore their gates. If I brought the Stone of Fál to Lunete or left it somewhere she was likely to find it, it could be a game-changer for them. If something like this was within my reach, those lives would be better.

I took off my jacket, determining that it was probably safest I didn't touch the stone, and thinking of the mistakes that had happened so far. I was also painfully aware of the water it was sat in. The stone had obviously been placed here for a reason.

When I reached the edge after climbing down the beige-grey rock, I left my lantern on the ground behind me and tested the water depth with the edge of my boot. They were sturdy with thick rubber soles, and it was the only thing around me that might've helped anyway. Whilst it ran over the curve of my shoe, I was still able to walk its depth. At first, I was gentle, but then, as my foot grew cold, I thought that speed would mean less chance of something happening.

My steps rippled and I could hear the lapping against the rock behind me. It wasn't far and I readied myself to reach for it, my hands restricted by the jacket. I couldn't be sure if what happened next was after I touched the stone or if there was something in the water. But before I knew it, the earth opened up beneath me and the water sucked me under.

• • • •

Above me, the colour of the rock shifted in the water's reflections. The very fabric of what I saw through a haze stretched and twisted vertically and horizontally at the same time. I thought my body was moving with it, and I couldn't tell if I was living in moments from my memories or hopping through my actual life. It felt like the veils between realms were so thin, I could simply reach through. But I wasn't the only one there. Time was non-existent and the fantastical became tangible, until I awoke, underwater.

I started, small bubbles escaping my mouth as I found my bearings.

Tall figures rose up all around me, and I had to force myself not to breathe the water in. I couldn't stay underwater for much longer and clawed my way to the surface regardless of what was waiting for me out there. I was not struck senseless by the dark's attack this time, and in some ways, I knew it better. It lived on instinct, and the darkness was being used like a tool by the Unseelie. Like I was.

I broke the surface, kicking weakly to find myself surrounded by a forest. At first, I couldn't be sure if it wasn't the same forest Pelthas was in, but as I lunged for the edge, I saw that the mosses and vines were a little too dense, the trees were too vibrant. My nails dug into the dirt as I tried to haul myself out from the lake. Arms shaking and knees not that much better, I couldn't stop heaving the air into my lungs. My chest ached.

As I laid in the grass, bone-weary, I also realised I must have dropped the stone and groaned. Curious about where I'd ended this time, and whether there was a chance to recover it, I pushed myself up, swaying, shivering. I pushed my back up against a nearby rock. The air was not cold, but I could only assume it was from the water that clung to me.

Sunlight cast through the dense canopy above, a mosaic of light and shadow on the forest floor. Through the clearing, smaller shrubs pervaded the spaces amongst the trees. Ancient trees were adorned with lichens and moss, their leaves silent in the still air. There was no-one else around, and as I tried to listen for any background roads or signs of life, I could feel the panic build up in my chest. Whilst there wasn't even birdsong, potential clung to everything around me, and I would've been foolish to treat it any differently than the cavern before. As the dappled beauty felt too peaceful, I remembered the vision I'd had with Eoghan and Lunete, and that liminal space. A different part of me was struck by the possibility that my life might be over and there was no one to help. Could the time rift even be restored now?

The longer I sat there, the more I began to notice the subtle discrepancies in what was around me. Leaves I thought were lush and green bore hints of decay, hues of yellow and brown mottling their edges. The ivy and vines were twisted and thick, scarring the ancient tree trunks and suffocating the life within.

The silence gathered a thickness and grew heavy, it reminded me of how the darkness formed in my peripheries. Tell-tale signs of some kind of infection revived my uneasiness, though I was hesitant to leave. I could have explored and tried to see where I was, I could have tried to find anything that might have helped, food, shelter, but I knew for certain I had arrived here. I had travelled again. So I knew I would have to go in the water again.

I waited until my heart settled, long enough that I'd expected some change in the light, but by the time I hesitantly stood, there had been no change in the shadows around me. My plan, even if I couldn't use the waters like the times before, was to see if the Stone of Fál had come with me. If it had, all of this wouldn't have been a complete waste of time.

I waded slowly, finding my footing on the stones before crouching down to submerge my wet clothes again. It was cold, shockingly, lifelessly cold, and my teeth began to rattle again. When I was confident it wasn't going to transport me anywhere, I took a few deep breaths to prepare my lungs, and I dropped haltingly until the water pressed in on me from every direction. Blood pounded in my ears as I blinked a few times to see through the blur of water.

It was murky, the dirt I'd kicked up from walking formed a cloud before me. Like the forest, there didn't appear to be any life. Pulling myself through slowly, I let the haze settle and headed towards the area I thought I'd come from. There were no weeds, no drifting green strands. I surfaced for air, my lungs already tired from before, and found myself near the middle of the lake. The eroded bank rose and made a ledge on the other side. I hadn't done much more than touch the waters previously but had to turn my focus back to the stone first. I would worry about getting back next.

Taking another deep breath, I ducked under again, heading closer to what I could see of the bottom. I scouted the mud, looking for anything the right kind of size or colour. I poked a few rocks amongst the leaf litter and sticks, checking their shape. The water had only cleared so much, an underwater storm, and it was only when I saw the canyon open up underneath me that I felt something brush my leg.

I grabbed the stone I'd been about to look at, my instinct knowing I was vulnerable. I twisted, driving myself to the surface again, adrenaline hammering through me. I nearly gasped and attempted to see which direction it had been, had I actually felt something? Over the edge of the underwater ravine, the foggy water faded to black. Somewhere at the back of my mind, I knew my time was running out.

My need for air was spreading. I cast another look about me and began pulling myself towards shore again. I needed to breathe. When something grasped my ankle, and dragged me down.

Chapter
Twenty-Seven

As soon as it happened, I knew I was among those whom the darkness preyed upon. It was a different feeling to being at the house— time was existent and life, the real world, was tangible. I had been here before though. It was a connection I could use. I could feel who it was keeping its grip on, who it had been told to watch, where it extended itself. It squirmed and coiled, not understanding why it felt pain, not knowing where its discomfort came from.

A sprawling city that could have been Falias, the place of resonant energy it had been told to feed on, erupted. It was like a dream again; things were familiar, but I could still only watch. People in green uniform pushed the shadow's limbs—the guards it had influence over—into the surrounding streets and alleys. The darkness watched a lean white dog that looked remarkably like Oona run through the ferns and bracken, except this one paused briefly to howl, a chorus from its throat, and a minute later, it was joined by three others. They hunted together, synchronised and intelligent. The shadow felt some of the fear it had caused in others and felt the need to hide.

The woman with long black hair spoke quickly through a tense jaw, her fury directed at the one who often directed the shadow. He looked my way, and I couldn't be sure if he was seeing me or the shadow. I couldn't make out her words, but her hands raised in betrayal. The bald male looked past her, not caring or not listening. The white-haired female watched from a corner, shadows holding her, bound by the very limbs I was watching.

The sight of Lunete jarred me, and my lucidity returned.

And with it, the control I ultimately had of my own life. I tried to recall the peace I'd felt when I held the stone.

I felt the rock I still physically had in my hand and angled my aim at the numbness creeping into my calf. My smash was water-logged but struck something that felt like oil, slippery and thick. Its smoky nature was at odds with the grip it had on me. It shifted, but it wrapped around me again as soon as it had let go. My chest ached the second time that day, and I frantically clawed and kicked my way back to shallower waters. Feeling torn between two depths, I managed to draw in another breath before I was pulled back under, its grip travelling up my leg. Urgency guided me, and I reached into the coiling mass of black weeds, desperate to rip it off. One of its limbs wrapped around my wrist, almost as if it struggled in my grip as much as I struggled in its grip.

Without being dragged down, I scrambled back into shallow waters, the light broke through the gloom, and as soon as one of my feet got onto the ground, the creature let go. Squirming, it retreated into deeper waters and disappeared again.

This time, as I gathered myself shivering, a cry escaped my throat. The entirety of it all ripped into my core— where I was, how I was going to get back, the whereabouts of the stone, the feeling of another threat, something I knew I should be thinking about but just couldn't. Watching the direction of the lake, I had to rest my head on my knees and gather myself. I felt drained, a husk, and I didn't know how a husk would be able to change anything.

It looked as if no time had passed on shore. There were still no shadows, and the light showed no sign of shifting. I hadn't seen shadows that the darkness seemed to appear from, and it hadn't slithered out onto the bank yet, but I didn't want to let my guard drop either. The feeling of dread was heavy in my gut.

Stretching my legs, I tried to walk around the clearing to steady my breathing. Whilst I hadn't seen any threats there yet, I hadn't seen any other life either. The canopies were still silent and there wasn't any rustling at all. It took on an eerie tone as I walked, and the feeling that I was the only one around heightened. My options grew clearer the more footprints were left in the dirt behind me. If I didn't try again, I would be compelled to live or die with these trees. And whilst that was tempting to a part of me, I also noted that I would never find this lake and my old life again if I left to find food. If there was even anything edible here.

I could stay safe on shore, survive perhaps, but I would never do anything.

Filtered rays of light pierced through the canopy, disturbing the fog that lay over the lake and illuminated patches of natural beauty. Delicate flowers, defiant against the encroaching rot, continued to bloom. Speckle-headed families of toadstools provided a stark contrast to the decay of ancient trunks and leaves. And I knew I'd have to go back in.

• • • •

It was now or never. I took some deep breaths, steeling myself, expanding my lungs, and swam in again.

Determined, I headed down to where it had found me before. I wanted it over with. I was in the position to help, and I was only holding myself back. It hadn't liked me grabbing it, and it hadn't liked the shallower waters. It almost didn't seem possible that I'd actually be able to hurt it, or kill it, as I only had certain tools there. As the surface light faded, nothing grasped me this time. The air I held inside quickly became stale, but when I left myself time to float back up, my head was still angled underwater, watching the depths below.

I didn't want to be caught off guard again. The surface broke, and I immediately refreshed my breath. Twice more I dived under and scouted the sides around the crevice. My lungs ached more and more with every resurface, and I didn't want to be caught in a position of hopelessness again.

Until it was there, all of a sudden, lurking in a cracked rock that could've been any other piece of darkness. I might have completely missed it the first time, however, the more I examined it through a squinted gaze, the more it shifted. It knew when I knew and, instead of remaining hidden, it struck out at me again.

Seizing my wrist before I had time to react, it drifted like oil in water, dissipating into the deep water behind it. I grappled with it in return, catching it with my other hand as I tried to edge closer to where it was thickest. The water around it was chilled, and its oily grip squeezed back so hard that the numbness I'd expected began to hurt. It writhed back at my attack, the struggle pulling at my skin, forcing me to release a few bubbles of air. Bracing myself, my fear as alive as the mass in my hands, I reached towards its centre and wrapped my hand around something semi-solid.

It leapt my way, further onto me, pushing me through the water. It made tangles around my hands and webs of my arms. I kicked towards the surface, out of breath, and regretted not having a better plan. It clutched my arms tighter and tighter, challenging me to give up control again. I couldn't go through it all again, but still didn't know what to do now the moment was here.

I became desperate again, my need for fresh air thumping in my head. I couldn't tell if the shadow was beginning to obscure what I was seeing, where darkness floated around the edges of my vision. In a last effort to break the water, I kicked hard and plunged my teeth into the vine-like limbs wrapped around my arms. Bitter oil filled my mouth, leaving an acrid trail down my throat. It clouded my vision further as it rose around me in the water, stinging my eyes. I had to make an effort not to choke until I was out of the water.

It tightened on me again and felt like scalding metal braces. I bit hard again and again, chewing through the pieces I needed to dislodge. It tensed and contorted, but the surface finally broke over us, and my body seemed to know before I did as my lungs filled with air. My head immediately felt unsupported, too light, and I had to focus on the squirming in my hands.

Still half submerged in the lake, outside the water the shadow dissipated, like the ones I'd run from. Chest heaving, legs shaking, I stumbled back to where the water was paddling depth. The shadow continued disintegrating in the light, leaving deep welts behind on my arms and hands. Coughing finally as my immediate need for fresh breath faded, I wiped my mouth to find the back of my hand painted with the darkness I'd just been choking on.

The clearing was still quiet, unnaturally so, and I didn't realise until my splashing footsteps faded away from me. The sound of the water around me, the sound of my coughing, and collapsing, was lost in the silence. The water had risen up to meet me, but I had no strength left to push it away. It was shallow enough to rest for a short while.

Chapter
Twenty-Eight

The woman with long black hair and another came into view. The man had yellow hair and remained a few steps behind as she paced. Somewhere at the back of my mind, I knew it was the entrance guarded by the shadow, the one I had passed through earlier to get to the cave. The shadow dissipated into their lanterns, and four other figures stood further back.

"My Lady," the yellow-haired man said, "it will poison me in its current state. I won't be able to do anything."

"Well, if you'd only been able to reach out to the stone when you had a chance," she jeered, and then held her hand out to one of the other figures. "T'sol, I need you. What's happening? Why are you weakening?"

The bald male, T'sol I could recognise, was reluctant to come closer. I could see he wasn't standing tall anymore, his pace was slow and pained. "I won't be able to do anything, she's beyond all of us now."

"So that's it for you? After all these years?" Neasa slashed at the darkness, testing it, but she moved through it as if she were the ghost. It reminded me of when I'd tried to help Lunete. "I will do what my father couldn't."

Another figure cautiously entered the line of light, silent and delicate on her feet. Lunete whispered hastily to T'sol, "What does she mean? Who was her father?"

231

One of the guards pushed her, minding her position. It felt too tense for the narrow space, concentrated to the point where some small comment could be the ignition. Through the rock, the muffled sounds of fighting, shouts, and screams added to the agitation.

"You have already achieved so much." T'sol stepped forward again, his hand finding the wall for support. "Neasa, look at what we've achieved."

"We have achieved nothing! You—" She raised her finger in accusation. "I never should have trusted that you could carry this."

"A daughter orphaned from the last war... You're Llyr's daughter," Lunete said quietly, I nearly didn't hear her over the rising echoes carried down the hallways. "You planned all this from the beginning."

T'sol turned suddenly, glancing between his sister and his childhood friend. He lowered his voice. "Lunete, I want you to hear me when I say that I didn't know for certain when I was a boy and let her into our home."

Lunete didn't have time to respond before Neasa laughed, still trying to find a way through. "You weren't without your suspicions." Then, pacing, she turned her eyes from the shadow to Lunete. "Your father drove him right to me. For all his noble words, he couldn't stand that his heir had more drive than he did."

The other man seemed to be the only one aware of the situation outside their bickering. He turned his senses on the noises above and slowly moved past T'sol and Lunete, directing the henchmen stationed further down the tunnel. Angling himself side on, he appeared to still be involved with whatever else was unravelling.

Behind me the darkness continued to distort, contracting. I could feel it struggling to stay present, and even though my life would be much easier without the darkness, I held onto it. I used it, needing to know what was going to happen. Some part of me was aware that they were close-by, but I also knew that I must be unconscious somewhere. Though T'sol tried to hide it, his face increasingly folded in pain, his limbs became as tense as the coils blocking their way to the stone.

"You have no idea what deciphering signs is like," Lunete replied. "The council that suspected my brother is the same council that interpreted the way to stop your father."

Neasa stopped, her eyes still focused on the other. Her stillness added a depth to her expression, her eyes narrowed. "I'd been too young to fully understand where my father's plan had gone wrong. All these years, I'd thought there'd been something he had overlooked, when really... you mean I could've plunged a knife in your little heart as soon as T'sol let me in?"

Before T'sol's weakened form could get between them, before my spectral presence could even try to help, Neasa moved to catch her. An intricate knife clutched against Lunete's throat. If she felt fear, her white eyes didn't show it as her face became more impassive than Neasa's. Her expression knowing.

Metal clashes and shouts rung down the hallway, closing them into the space.

"My Lady?" the man called to Neasa, asking for direction. Deftly, he detached a handful of sharp flat metal shards from his belt and, after looking back to check if there was any objection, started throwing them into the conflict.

Neasa's mouth still moved, the words too low for me to hear. Lunete seemed to be keeping her talking. The noise emerged from the tunnel and became distant shapes, guarding the commanders who fought other figures. There was a press, henchmen backs and the wounded penned us in, until a line of familiar uniforms broke into view.

T'sol cried out, doubling over, whatever connection that brought the darkness into creation reversing. I felt the shadow recede. I watched as he retched, the same blackness I'd choked on painting the back of his hand. In the same way lucidity returned in a dream, I could feel the shadow dying, desperately still drawing on those still under its influence. I would wake up somewhere any moment soon.

Breaking past the Unseelie that were still fighting, the figures in green leather parted and checked on those bleeding against the same walls I'd traced earlier. Neasa grew frantic, her attention split; the life she'd just found out she wanted still in her hands.

"Release her!" One of the commanders stepped towards them, hand raised, though I didn't know if it was in peace or defence.

Neasa shoved her into the rock again, the blood from under her knife-edge beginning to stain her white hair.

She was immediately struck in the shoulder by a heavy bolt, the force of it driving her into Lunete further. Olwen strode out from the parted guards, crossbow still trained on Neasa.

In the mess of blood and once fine clothes, Neasa manoeuvred behind her hostage to look Lunete's twin in the eyes. Though they were still standing, she slumped against the same wall. She struggled, holding herself up with her knife-hand slung around Lunete's shoulder as her other arm hung limply. The bolt, I could then see, had pierced her shoulder blade and most likely a lung. T'sol lay still, slumped between where I felt I was and the women.

"We reclaim Falias in the name of the Seelie," Olwen said as calmly as her sister, her voice solid in the sudden quiet. "You don't have to make things worse for yourself."

Without truly realising it, I felt like I skipped a minute as I blearily saw Neasa shift again and Olwen shout.

Chapter
Twenty-Nine

Muffled noises woke me again. Only it wasn't just muffled. I was underwater, but the closeness wasn't suffocating this time.

Arms looped mine, and the air was cold when we surfaced. The sleep I was on the edge of would be broken if I acknowledged the world and breathed. Was I still in the woods?

"Eoghan!" I heard a familiar voice splutter from next to me as the back of my legs hit the lakebed. "She's not breathing! That looks like the same darkness that killed T'sol."

I was laid down, the warmth of the chest I'd been against faded into the rock. I felt them check my pulse and the temperature of my skin. One gently opened my left eye, but I couldn't focus. The outline was indistinct against the light that filled the space behind them.

"I should think the old magic would have sustained her," the same voice said. Was that Drust?

"It has. She's still alive, but the darkness has infected her," Eoghan replied. "Was the stone still there? It'd be best to retrieve it for the time being, and break anything the Unseelie has arranged." Then, after I heard the splash of water again. "Oh Morgan, these things are so unpredictable. I'm sorry, I don't know of any other way. Things like this demand balance."

The next thing I knew, stale air filled my lungs, my body desperate for oxygen. I coughed, head spinning, and turned to face the rock. A vile mixture of bile, black oil, and water sloshed out of me and hit the dirt below. My whole body ached, and the realness of the situation set my blood racing in panic. A short distance away, I recognised Freda's features, though I hadn't seen her since we were at the house. She was looking my way but stood with a group of guards who watched the hallway entrance. Had that been real? What had happened to Lunete?

My body swayed, weak. The carved arches and worn statues that cleared in my vision added a strange sense of relief though. They were all here. They had been able to travel somehow too. The faint scent of earth rose to meet me as what little energy I had left disappeared.

When I finally awoke, the bustle of voices and cries met my ears. Urgent requests and conversations from the reunited were occasionally lost in the expressions of pain. As I stirred, the musk of turmeric and marigold permeated the air heavily like a fog, and occasionally, busy helpers broke the air with something like tea tree. Cots and makeshift beds lined every wall, with the odd chair squeezed in the spaces between. Around me, the injured laid in every type of armour I'd seen so far. Soldiers from both courts, adversaries only days ago, were tended together with skilled hands and words of comfort. The animosity and selfishness momentarily forgotten in the shared understanding of pain.

I felt surprisingly refreshed. I knew there were things I should remember, but they felt intangible.

"Morgan? Are you with us?" Drust's familiar figure came into focus, he sat forward in one of the chairs. His dark eyebrows were straight, rising in the centre and betraying his concern.

"Drust?" My voice was hoarse, and I had to use volume to break any sound through. "What happened? Is Áine with you?"

With my response, he closed whatever work he'd been doing, leaving it on the chair behind him, and helped me sit up. My limbs felt clumsy among the soft fabrics that had been collected and patchworked.

"We'll explain what's gone on. Áine's safe at Pelthas. How do you feel?"

"Surprisingly clear, and lucky, given where we are."

"That's good." He watched me as if he might catch something I was hiding. "What do you remember?"

As I cast my memory back, the reminder of certain events was enough to trigger the feeling that I'd witnessed something important.

"I remember accidentally finding the stone... it took me somewhere... I remember the darkness, and Neasa and... Lunete. Is she—"

Drust lowered his voice and briefly cast a look around the ward. "The Seelie Council are all alive and the Unseelie were subdued, but T'sol and the Unseelie woman were beyond helping. I believe that as T'sol was the wielder, the shadow's life force was linked with his own." He hesitated for a second before continuing. "Whatever you were able to do to restore the gates infected you too..."

"Where's Eoghan?" I asked. "Surely there can't be any doubt about his exile now?"

"I think you know by now that there are certain rules we have to follow and he... was determined to save you." My heart grew heavy suddenly and pulled at my throat. Any warmth I still had gathered behind my eyes as Drust continued.

"It was too late by the time I got back to you. He wanted you to know that this is how your parents would've had it, and that he was proud of you."

The same confusion and obscurity I'd felt during my time in Falias returned, and I didn't know what to say when I felt like I barely knew him. I knew I would miss his presence though.

I felt a gentle warmth on my arm and found Drust there, bringing me back to the present. "Whatever you decide to do with your life will be enough. No one has any expectations, Morgan, only you can decide what will make your life worth living. The simple fact is not even Lunete knows for certain what will happen in the future. It could all shift again, but if it does, we can just change direction with it." He watched me, uncertain of how I was taking the news. "I'll be right back, okay? I need to let the physician know you're awake."

He waited a moment after standing, as if giving me a chance to speak, and made his way through the busy chamber. He scanned the aides, between families and beds in the same clothing, until he found an available one.

I looked around at the various states of suffering. There were limbs and heads wrapped in bleached bandages, and many also looked shell shocked. Were they coming out of their own fog? I knew certain events must have happened but, in my mind, they were dim and half-lived. For the first time, I thought about the stories those ancient ceilings could tell, and the secrets I might find buried in some of the rooms here. My life was open, and I didn't know what I wanted it to look like, but that held its own freedom. I felt what their court could be— a mutual respect for every being's needs.

My fingers wandered to my pocket. They met the outline of my van's key, and instead of thinking of the escape she offered me, I felt the support instead. It was always there if I needed to go back to it. I checked my pocket again for the other brass key but found nothing. Hopefully there was a spare if it opened anything important.

Shortly after the physician had checked in and asked me to stay a few more hours to make sure, Drust spoke about Eoghan's idea of confirming what had happened, and where I was, and how the council had reacted to Lunete's subsequent abduction. They had mobilised soon after, and when the alerts had gone out to say the gates were active again, assailed to take back the city.

He spotted Olwen, Belenus, and a pair of guards soon after as they made their way through the ward. They gradually drew closer, Olwen doing her part as figurehead, offering words of strength and sympathies to those who called her. By the time they reached us, they seemed to relax. Belenus gave a great sigh, and though Olwen's eyes were lined with weariness, there was an unwavering dedication in her set brow. Unbidden, the memory of her cry when Lunete was in danger rang through my head. At the same time, in my conscious state, I unexpectedly realised what T'sol had done in making our Pact and needed to make sure they were aware.

"You're no doubt getting tired of this question," Belenus said, "but the healer said you might be on the path to recovery?"

I nodded, sitting forward, "I feel better than I have in months, it's still so foggy though."

"We have reason to believe the Unseelie found a way to influence you whilst you were under our care. We owe you our apologies and gratitude," Olwen said, lowering her voice slightly. "It can be difficult herding the minds of the council, and if they had acted any slower, I could have found myself without a sister as well."

"I'm sorry I had no way of helping her. How is she? I didn't know what I was agreeing to before it was too late."

"Recovering but alive." She paused, swallowing, before saying, "It's not yet clear if she'll be able to speak again. The Unseelie have much to answer for, but I know it's not always that simple." Her eyes flicked to Drust and I knew she wondered who else had been exploited.

"I don't want to overstep, but I do think there was a part of T'sol that struggled against Neasa." I hesitated, continuing only when Olwen tilted her head in interest. "Though I wasn't able to help Lunete, once I'd found that place, I don't think Neasa was able to interfere either. Maybe he was trying in his own way to atone?"

They took this in. Belenus scoffed as he said, "I really don't think there can be amends for patricide."

But Olwen glanced between us and looked thoughtful. "We're still sorting through the rubble and organising what we can. We might find the Pact if there was one. We should see more people now, but we wanted to let you know there'll be a memorial for everyone who fell. It's in a couple of days."

"I'll be there." They moved to go when I added, "Could I quickly ask if there's any news about when the gates will be safe to use?"

Belenus nodded. "Probably not long after. It gives us time to make sure nothing else has changed. There are still groups of Unseelie who haven't received the message, but there's no need to keep the ones we retained locked. Even your father's if you're willing. There's also the matter of the time discrepancy, now the rift has been restored. Even if you stayed until the end of the year, you'll find that a couple of years will have passed."

"What will happen to the gate if I don't look after it?" I asked Drust after they moved on.

"You mean if Oona will let them?" He smirked and raised a brow in thought. "That one's your family's by right, but until you say otherwise, they'll probably start to track down another gatekeeper heir to minimise travel disruption."

"And Eoghan's home? All his work?"

"Well, whomever he left it to. It's not the Seelies' to claim."

Chapter Thirty

O n the day of the memorial, I was reminded of the caverns on Ēostre. It had been about half a year since then. As we made our way through the crowds of people, Drust and I arrived at the largest city square I'd seen yet. He'd visited the places his parents might've sheltered and returned a little more impenetrable each time. The only way I could help was to gently remind him that it was a big city, someone would have seen something, and he hadn't found any news yet.

At the sides and down back streets, I could still see the remnants of broken carts and boxes, ashy marks scarred the stonework, but it had been transformed into a remembrance. In my own way, whilst I'd helped clear away debris and wash down walls, I'd tried to keep up with the fragile conversations that emerged in the streets. I willed any news to surface— about his parents, about the one who'd given me small tokens, about Hazel's family.

Whilst the afternoon was missing the laughter and children playing from before, people stood talking together, and others listened to hand-carved instruments on the side of the street. The foundations of a bonfire laid at the centre of spiralled paving. Tributes were added around the three-storey buildings that lined the perimeter of the square, surrounding the crowd that had already gathered. Different families of Aspects had left drawings, letters, food, and clothes of the lost.

As we stood in the hushed crowd gathered in the plaza, the weight of their struggles was unmistakable. The air was thick with grief but the faces around me carried it together. We had come together to remember and hope for a brighter future. Olwen, Lunete, Belenus, and Agrona stood on a raised platform to one side, clad in the same tough green leathers that guarded their perimeter. Lunete had a clean white dressing wrapped around her throat.

The council stepped forward. Olwen's voice was strong and clear as she addressed the crowd. Her words carried the authority of those who'd guided the Seelie for generations and their hope that future generations would embrace what they made together.

"People of the Seelie Court, we gather here today not only to remember those who recently fell but to also acknowledge my family's role in these events." A solemn hush fell over the crowd as her words sank in.

"There are so many yet unaccounted for, and we want to emphasise, if you're looking for anyone, if there are shadows in your memories, please find a member of the Second Council. Those that have been identified, we honour now. Our fallen brothers and sisters endured the end, and we will not forget them."

As their names were recited, some faces were solemn, some were tearful, some had their eyes closed, and some recited the names after her. The silence that held us invoked a moment of shared sorrow, a collective grieving for what had been lost. When she spoke Eoghan's name, his Master status had been restored.

When her speech continued, it was also a promise for a new path ahead. "We acknowledge the responsibility that lies upon us. Our brother's actions brought suffering and division, and we must confront this painful truth. In the wake of this devastating conflict, we recognise the need for a new Pact. With the spirit of peace, let us remember that the strength of Albios lies not in our differences, but in our ability to come together. May this new Pact be a testament to our resilience and create a world where understanding flourishes for all."

Epilogue

Passing back through Pelthas, I saw Áine and the girls before they headed the other way. She was nervous but relieved to be able to settle with her sisters again. Drust had said he'd visit, but he had obligations in Falias first.

I had to call breakdown recovery for my van on the first roadside phone near the car park I'd left her in. The fact that it hadn't been clamped or towed was just a testament to how hidden Pelthas was. I ignored my paranoia when the looks I received from the mechanic asked me different questions to the ones coming from their mouth. They asked what I thought the problem was, but their look asked how my van looked so run down in comparison to my freshened state. When they asked where I was heading, their eyes darted to the lean canine figure that sat primly a short distance away.

Oona had joined me shortly after I'd left the caverns. As entities of subjective loyalties, she and her pack hadn't joined the final engagement, but she'd waited patiently for me on the other side. I chatted with her when we were back on the road, asking her if she was planning on staying with me. I peered at her in my rearview mirror, back to the bed covered in blankets at the back of my van. She laid in a crescent shape, eyes on mine over the little kitchenette, and moved her head from one paw to the other in response.

I travelled on to my father's house shortly after, clouds as mottled as the day I'd first arrived. Despite Eoghan's sacrifice for me, I could still feel the remnants of the darkness at the back of my mind. After hearing my account, Drust and Master

Enid both thought the shadow couldn't live without T'sol, but also couldn't say if I'd feel like this the rest of my life. Before I left, Drust had said it was something he had to manage and learnt how to live with it.

The hours slipped by when I was on the road, but it was joined by the contentment it always gave me. When I arrived, fresh weeds reached between different paved stones that led to the familiar door, whilst layers of present and future foliage pressed into the path. Ivy and mildew still hadn't touched the house, and now I knew they wouldn't. At first, I knew I would go back and visit Olivia and Joanne and I meant to use the house as a rest stop, but as I pulled onto the street, it felt more homely to me now than the small, terrace house Mum and I had shared.

Don't be a stranger, be safe!

Hope you get signal some time, missing you x

Happy birthday! Got cake and wine, if you don't, why not? x

Is it too late to set up a backup plan? Let me know you're okay x

When you get back, we're setting up checkpoints and secret passwords if this is happening again.

Morgan, me and Joanne are thinking of contacting the police, we just want to know you're alive. We'll give you another day.

All right, happy? You're a missing person, the police searched that town you were at and couldn't find any evidence of where you went next. Please come home, it's not the same without you.

When my phone connected and caught up, I felt sick as every notification laid a sense of accountability on my mind. It hadn't been a whole year, but without a way to charge my phone, there hadn't been any other way to check in.

I looked around, into my father's office, where his books and papers were still piled on the sofa where we'd left them, and down the hall into the kitchen, where we'd begun to piece together what was happening around the breakfast bar. Oona nosed past me, and she reacquainted herself by fervently sniffing the empty rooms. As if I was on borrowed time before letting the world know I was still alive, before apologising profusely to Olivia and hoping she'd let me back in her life, I slowly walked over to the door that protected the gate. Whilst I knew Freda and a support team had stayed behind to make sure it was kept safe, and whilst I knew I wouldn't be stalked any longer, the simple oak frame gave me pause.

Stepping forward, I raised my hand. The wood wasn't cold and hummed in the same way the tunnel walls had. Like the feeling that struck me the first time or that of touching the stone, it was empowering to know I had control over the life and energy running through my veins. My fingers ran over the grain towards the lever handle and pushed it open.

· · · ·

My dearest Morgan,

I hope this letter finds you well and safe. I know it has been well over a month for you and not even a week for us, but you have been in all of our thoughts. Ruari and Emer have been asking when you'll visit again.

The city is still recovering and we all look forward to the rest, food, and celebrations at the end of the day. In full Seelie spirit, we support each other and know the streets will be vibrant again.

I found what remains of our home and was able to salvage some of our family's belongings. I hope it will make a new home easier for the girls.

I know Drust is visiting at the end of your month (a couple of days for us here!) and I'm sure he'll tell you all about it, but he may need your strength. He has found his parents but only time can heal them now. Your joint request to go through what Eoghan left you and continue his research is looking positive though. The council has begun narrowing down possible gatekeepers to continue your tutelage too. I saw Hazel when she came in to speak to them.

Now that tensions are beginning to settle, my role as a diplomat has been needed again. The Second Council that I'm part of have been working tirelessly to patch the rift between the courts. We're hoping this new Pact will last longer than a generation... it's not going to be easy, of course, but it's what our people deserve. The council have also received emissaries from neighbouring races and communities, which falls to us as well. The outreach of support and recognition has been heartening, even though they were threatened too.

Despite all this, I'm so pleased you've decided to take up your father's post (and I know Drust is too, but you didn't hear that from me), and we'll be going on explorations before you know it.

Until then, you're in our hearts, look after yourself,
Áine.

About the Author

As a lifelong writer and inkdrinker, Lucy works as a library assistant and studies English Literature & Language part-time. Read more at www.instagram.com/longhand.hearted.

Printed in Great Britain
by Amazon

48303648R00148